BREAKING SILENCE

DELTA FORCE STRONG BOOK #1

ELLE JAMES

TWISTED PAGE INC

BREAKING SILENCE

DELTA FORCE STRONG BOOK #1

New York Times & *USA Today*
Bestselling Author

ELLE JAMES

ISBN-13: 978-1-62695-325-3 (Ebook)

ISBN-13: 978-1-62695-329-1 (Paperback)

Dedicated to all the men and women in uniform: Army, Air Force, Navy, Marines and law enforcement. Thank you for your service!
Elle James

AUTHOR'S NOTE

Enjoy other military books by Elle James

Delta Force Strong
Ivy's Delta (Delta Force 3 Crossover)
Breaking Silence (#1)
Breaking Rules (#2)
Breaking Away (#3)
Breaking Free (#4)
Breaking Hearts (#5)

Brotherhood Protectors Colorado
SEAL Salvation (#1)
Rocky Mountain Rescue (#2)
Ranger Redemption (#3)
Tactical Takeover (#4)
Shadow Assassin (crossover)

Visit ellejames.com for more titles and release dates
For hot cowboys, visit her alter ego Myla Jackson at
mylajackson.com
and join Elle James's Newsletter at
https://ellejames.com/contact/

CHAPTER 1

HAD he known they would be deployed so soon after their last short mission to El Salvador, Rucker Sloan wouldn't have bought that dirt bike from his friend Duff. Now, it would sit there for months before he actually got to take it out to the track.

The team had been given forty-eight hours to pack their shit, take care of business and get onto the C130 that would transport them to Afghanistan.

Now, boots on the ground, duffel bags stowed in their assigned quarters behind the wire, they were ready to take on any mission the powers that be saw fit to assign.

What he wanted most that morning, after being awake for the past thirty-six hours, was a cup of strong, black coffee.

The rest of his team had hit the sack as soon as they got in. Rucker had already met with their commanding officer, gotten a brief introduction to the regional issues and had been told to get some rest. They'd be operational within the next forty-eight hours.

Too wound up to sleep, Rucker followed a stream of people he hoped were heading for the chow hall. He should be able to get coffee there.

On the way, he passed a sand volleyball court where two teams played against each other. One of the teams had four players, the other only three. The four-person squad slammed a ball to the ground on the other side of the net. The only female player ran after it as it rolled toward Rucker.

He stopped the ball with his foot and picked it up.

The woman was tall, slender, blond-haired and blue-eyed. She wore an Army PT uniform of shorts and an Army T-shirt with her hair secured back from her face in a ponytail seated on the crown of her head.

Without makeup, and sporting a sheen of perspiration, she was sexy as hell, and the men on both teams knew it.

They groaned when Rucker handed her the ball. He'd robbed them of watching the female soldier bending over to retrieve the runaway.

She took the ball and frowned. "Do you play?"

"I have," he answered.

"We could use a fourth." She lifted her chin in challenge.

Tired from being awake for the past thirty-six hours, Rucker opened his mouth to say *hell no*. But he made the mistake of looking into her sky-blue eyes and instead said, "I'm in."

What the hell was he thinking?

Well, hadn't he been wound up from too many hours sitting in transit? What he needed was a little physical activity to relax his mind and muscles. At least, that's what he told himself in the split-second it took to step into the sandbox and serve up a heaping helping of whoop-ass.

He served six times before the team playing opposite finally returned one. In between each serve, his side gave him high-fives, all members except one— the blonde with the blue eyes he stood behind, admiring the length of her legs beneath her black Army PT shorts.

Twenty minutes later, Rucker's team won the match. The teams broke up and scattered to get showers or breakfast in the chow hall.

"Can I buy you a cup of coffee?" the pretty blonde asked.

"Only if you tell me your name." He twisted his lips into a wry grin. "I'd like to know who delivered those wicked spikes."

She held out her hand. "Nora Michaels," she said.

He gripped her hand in his, pleased to feel firm pressure. Women might be the weaker sex, but he didn't like a dead fish handshake from males or females. Firm and confident was what he preferred. Like her ass in those shorts.

She cocked an eyebrow. "And you are?"

He'd been so intent thinking about her legs and ass, he'd forgotten to introduce himself. "Rucker Sloan. Just got in less than an hour ago."

"Then you could probably use a tour guide to the nearest coffee."

He nodded. "Running on fumes here. Good coffee will help."

"I don't know about good, but it's coffee and it's fresh." She released his hand and fell in step beside him, heading in the direction of some of the others from their volleyball game.

"As long as it's strong and black, I'll be happy."

She laughed. "And awake for the next twenty-four hours."

"Spoken from experience?" he asked, casting a glance in her direction.

She nodded. "I work nights in the medical facility. It can be really boring and hard to stay awake when we don't have any patients to look after." She held up her hands. "Not that I want any of our boys injured and in need of our care."

"But it does get boring," he guessed.

"It makes for a long deployment." She held out her hand. "Nice to meet you, Rucker. Is Rucker a call sign or your real name?"

He grinned. "Real name. That was the only thing

my father gave me before he cut out and left my mother and me to make it on our own."

"Your mother raised you, and you still joined the Army?" She raised an eyebrow. "Most mothers don't want their boys to go off to war."

"It was that or join a gang and end up dead in a gutter," he said. "She couldn't afford to send me to college. I was headed down the gang path when she gave me the ultimatum. Join and get the GI-Bill, or she would cut me off and I'd be out in the streets. To her, it was the only way to get me out of L.A. and to have the potential to go to college someday."

She smiled "And you stayed in the military."

He nodded. "I found a brotherhood that was better than any gang membership in LA. For now, I take college classes online. It was my mother's dream for me to graduate college. She never went, and she wanted so much more for me than the streets of L.A.. When my gig is up with the Army, if I haven't finished my degree, I'll go to college fulltime."

"And major in what?" Nora asked.

"Business management. I'm going to own my own security service. I want to put my combat skills to use helping people who need dedicated and specialized protection."

Nora nodded. "Sounds like a good plan."

"I know the protection side of things. I need to learn the business side and business law. Life will be different on the civilian side."

"True."

"How about you? What made you sign up?" he asked.

She shrugged. "I wanted to put my nursing degree to good use and help our men and women in uniform. This is my first assignment after training."

"Drinking from the firehose?" Rucker stopped in front of the door to the mess hall.

She nodded. "Yes. But it's the best baptism under fire medical personnel can get. I'll be a better nurse for it when I return to the States."

"How much longer do you have to go?" he asked, hoping that she'd say she'd be there as long as he was. In his case, he never knew how long their deployments would last. One week, one month, six months…

She gave him a lopsided smile. "I ship out in a week."

"That's too bad." He opened the door for her. "I just got here. That doesn't give us much time to get to know each other."

"That's just as well." Nora stepped through the door. "I don't want to be accused of fraternizing. I'm too close to going back to spoil my record."

Rucker chuckled. "Playing volleyball and sharing a table while drinking coffee won't get you written up. I like the way you play. I'm curious to know where you learned to spike like that."

"I guess that's reasonable. Coffee first." She led him into the chow hall.

The smells of food and coffee made Rucker's mouth water.

He grabbed a tray and loaded his plate with eggs, toast and pancakes drenched in syrup. Last, he stopped at the coffee urn and filled his cup with freshly brewed black coffee.

When he looked around, he found Nora seated at one of the tables, holding a mug in her hands, a small plate with cottage cheese and peaches on it.

He strode over to her. "Mind if I join you?"

"As long as you don't hit on me," she said with cocked eyebrows.

"You say that as if you've been hit on before."

She nodded and sipped her steaming brew. "I lost count how many times in the first week I was here."

"Shows they have good taste in women and, unfortunately, limited manners."

"And you're better?" she asked, a smile twitching the corners of her lips.

"I'm not hitting on you. You can tell me to leave, and I'll be out of this chair so fast, you won't have time to enunciate the V."

She stared straight into his eyes, canted her head to one side and said, "Leave."

In the middle of cutting into one of his pancakes, Rucker dropped his knife and fork on the tray, shot out of his chair and left with his tray, sloshing coffee as he moved. He hoped she was just testing him. If she wasn't…oh, well. He was used to eating meals alone. If she was, she'd have to come to him.

He took a seat at the next table, his back to her, and resumed cutting into his pancake.

Nora didn't utter a word behind him.

Oh, well. He popped a bite of syrupy sweet pancake in his mouth and chewed thoughtfully. She was only there for another week. Man, she had a nice ass…and those legs… He sighed and bent over his plate to stab his fork into a sausage link.

"This chair taken?" a soft, female voice sounded in front of him.

He looked up to see the pretty blond nurse standing there with her tray in her hands, a crooked smile on her face.

He lifted his chin in silent acknowledgement.

She laid her tray on the table and settled onto the chair. "I didn't think you'd do it."

"Fair enough. You don't know me," he said.

"I know that you joined the Army to get out of street life. That your mother raised you after your father skipped out, that you're working toward a business degree and that your name is Rucker." She sipped her coffee.

He nodded, secretly pleased she'd remembered all that. Maybe there was hope for getting to know the pretty nurse before she redeployed to the States. And who knew? They might run into each other on the other side of the pond.

Still, he couldn't show too much interest, or he'd be no better than the other guys who'd hit on her. "Since you're redeploying back to the States in a week, and I'm due to go out on a mission, probably within the next twenty-four to forty-eight hours, I don't know if it's worth our time to get to know each other any more than we already have."

She nodded. "I guess that's why I want to sit with you. You're not a danger to my perfect record of no fraternizing. I don't have to worry that you'll fall in love with me in such a short amount of time." She winked.

He chuckled. "As I'm sure half of this base has fallen in love with you since you've been here."

She shrugged. "I don't know if it's love, but it's damned annoying."

"How so?"

She rolled her eyes toward the ceiling. "I get flowers left on my door every day."

"And that's annoying? I'm sure it's not easy coming up with flowers out here in the desert." He set down his fork and took up his coffee mug. "I think it's sweet." He held back a smile. Well, almost.

"They're hand-drawn on notepad paper and left on the door of my quarters and on the door to the shower tent." She shook her head. "It's kind of creepy and stalkerish."

Rucker nodded. "I see your point. The guys should at least have tried their hands at origami flowers, since the real things are scarce around here."

Nora smiled. "I'm not worried about the pictures, but the line for sick call is ridiculous."

"How so?"

"So many of the guys come up with the lamest excuses to come in and hit on me. I asked to work the nightshift to avoid sick call altogether."

"You have a fan group." He smiled. "Has the adoration gone to your head?"

She snorted softly. "No."

"You didn't get this kind of reaction back in the States?"

"I haven't been on active duty for long. I only decided to join the Army after my mother passed away. I was her fulltime nurse for a couple years as she went through stage four breast cancer. We thought she might make it." Her shoulders sagged. "But she didn't."

"I'm sorry to hear that. My mother meant a lot to me, as well. I sent money home every month after I enlisted and kept sending it up until the day she died suddenly of an aneurysm."

"I'm so sorry about your mother's passing," Nora said, shaking her head. "Wow. As an enlisted man, how did you make enough to send some home?"

"I ate in the chow hall and lived on post. I didn't

party or spend money on civilian clothes or booze. Mom needed it. I gave it to her."

"You were a good son to her," Nora said.

His chest tightened. "She died of an aneurysm a couple of weeks before she was due to move to Texas where I'd purchased a house for her."

"Wow. And, let me guess, you blame yourself for not getting her to Texas sooner...?" Her gaze captured his.

Her words hit home, and he winced. "Yeah. I should've done it sooner."

"Can't bring people back with regrets." Nora stared into her coffee cup. "I learned that. The only thing I could do was move forward and get on with living. I wanted to get away from Milwaukee and the home I'd shared with my mother. Not knowing where else to go, I wandered past a realtor's office and stepped into a recruiter's office. I had my nursing degree, they wanted and needed nurses on active duty. I signed up, they put me through some officer training and here I am." She held her arms out.

"Playing volleyball in Afghanistan, working on your tan during the day and helping soldiers at night." Rucker gave her a brief smile. "I, for one, appreciate what you're doing for our guys and gals."

"I do the best I can," she said softly. "I just wish I could do more. I'd rather stay here than redeploy back to the States, but they're afraid if they keep us here too long, we'll burn out or get PTSD."

"One week, huh?"

She nodded. "One week."

"In my field, one week to redeploy back to the States is a dangerous time. Anything can happen and usually does."

"Yeah, but you guys are on the frontlines, if not behind enemy lines. I'm back here. What could happen?"

Rucker flinched. "Oh, sweetheart, you didn't just say that..." He glanced around, hoping no one heard her tempt fate with those dreaded words *What could happen?*

Nora grinned. "You're not superstitious, are you?"

"In what we do, we can't afford not to be," he said, tossing salt over his shoulder.

"I'll be fine," she said in a reassuring, nurse's voice.

"Stop," he said, holding up his hand. "You're only digging the hole deeper." He tossed more salt over his other shoulder.

Nora laughed.

"Don't laugh." He handed her the saltshaker. "Do it."

"I'm not tossing salt over my shoulder. Someone has to clean the mess hall."

Rucker leaned close and shook salt over her shoulder. "I don't know if it counts if someone else throws salt over your shoulder, but I figure you now need every bit of luck you can get."

"You're a fighter but afraid of a little bad luck."

Nora shook her head. "Those two things don't seem to go together."

"You'd be surprised how easily my guys are freaked by the littlest things."

"And you," she reminded him.

"You asking *what could happen?* isn't a little thing. That's in-your-face tempting fate." Rucker was laying it on thick to keep her grinning, but deep down, he believed what he was saying. And it didn't make a difference the amount of education he had or the statistics that predicted outcomes. His gut told him she'd just tempted fate with her statement. Maybe he was overthinking things. Now, he was worried she wouldn't make it back to the States alive.

NORA LIKED RUCKER. He was the first guy who'd walked away without an argument since she'd arrived at the base in Afghanistan. He'd meant what he'd said and proved it. His dark brown hair and deep green eyes, coupled with broad shoulders and a narrow waist, made him even more attractive. Not all the men were in as good a shape as Rucker. And he seemed to have a very determined attitude.

She hadn't known what to expect when she'd deployed. Being the center of attention of almost every single male on the base hadn't been one of her expectations. She'd only ever considered herself average in the looks department. But when the men outnumbered women by more than ten to one, she guessed average appearance moved up in the ranks.

"Where did you learn to play volleyball?" Rucker asked, changing the subject of her leaving and her flippant comment about what could happen in one week.

"I was on the volleyball team in high school. It got me a scholarship to a small university in my home state of Minnesota, where I got my Bachelor of Science degree in Nursing."

"It takes someone special to be a nurse," he stated. "Is that what you always wanted to be?"

She shook her head. "I wanted to be a firefighter when I was in high school."

"What made you change your mind?"

She stared down at the coffee growing cold in her mug. "My mother was diagnosed with cancer when I was a senior in high school. I wanted to help but felt like I didn't know enough to be of assistance." She looked up. "She made it through chemo and radiation treatments and still came to all of my volleyball games. I thought she was in the clear."

"She wasn't?" Rucker asked, his tone low and gentle.

"She didn't tell me any different. When I got the scholarship, I told her I wanted to stay close to home to be with her. She insisted I go and play volleyball for the university. I was pretty good and played for the first two years I was there. I quit the team in my third year to start the nursing program. I didn't know there was anything wrong back home. I called every week to talk to Mom. She never let on that she was sick." She forced a smile. "But you don't want my sob story. You probably want to know what's going on around here."

He set his mug on the table. "If we were alone in a coffee bar back in the States, I'd reach across the table and take your hand."

"Oh, please. Don't do that." She looked around the mess hall, half expecting someone might have overheard Rucker's comment. "You're enlisted. I'm an officer. That would get us into a whole lot of trouble."

"Yeah, but we're also two human beings. I wouldn't be human if I didn't feel empathy for you and want to provide comfort."

She set her coffee cup on the table and laid her hands in her lap. "I'll be satisfied with the thought. Thank you."

"Doesn't seem like enough. When did you find out your mother was sick?"

She swallowed the sadness that welled in her throat every time she remembered coming home to find out her mother had been keeping her illness from her. "It wasn't until I went home for Christmas in my senior year that I realized she'd been lying to me for a while." She laughed in lieu of sobbing. "I

15

don't care who they are, old people don't always tell the truth."

"How long had she been keeping her sickness from you?"

"She'd known the cancer had returned halfway through my junior year. I hadn't gone home that summer because I'd been working hard to get my coursework and clinical hours in the nursing program. When I went home at Christmas..." Nora gulped. "She wasn't the same person. She'd lost so much weight and looked twenty years older."

"Did you stay home that last semester?" Rucker asked.

"Mom insisted I go back to school and finish what I'd started. Like your mother, she hadn't gone to college. She wanted her only child to graduate. She was afraid that if I stayed home to take care of her, I wouldn't finish my nursing degree."

"I heard from a buddy of mine that those programs can be hard to get into," he said. "I can see why she wouldn't want you to drop everything in your life to take care of her."

Nora gave him a watery smile. "That's what she said. As soon as my last final was over, I returned to my hometown. I became her nurse. She lasted another three months before she slipped away."

"That's when you joined the Army?"

She shook her head. "Dad was so heartbroken, I stayed a few months until he was feeling better. I got a job at a local emergency room. On weekends, my father and I worked on cleaning out the house and getting it ready to put on the market."

"Is your dad still alive?" Rucker asked.

Nora nodded. "He lives in Texas. He moved to a small house with a big backyard." She forced a smile. "He has a garden, and all the ladies in his retirement community think he's the cat's meow. He still misses Mom, but he's getting on with his life."

Rucker tilted his head. "When did you join the military?"

"When Dad sold the house and moved into his retirement community. I worried about him, but he's doing better."

"And you?"

"I miss her. But she'd whip my ass if I wallowed in self-pity for more than a moment. She was a strong woman and expected me to be the same."

Rucker grinned. "From what I've seen, you are."

Nora gave him a skeptical look. "You've only seen me playing volleyball. It's just a game." Not that she'd admit it, but she was a real softy when it came to caring for the sick and injured.

"If you're half as good at nursing, which I'm willing to bet you are, you're amazing." He started to reach across the table for her hand. Before he actually touched her, he grabbed the saltshaker and shook it over his cold breakfast.

"You just got in this morning?" Nora asked.

Rucker nodded.

"How long will you be here?" she asked.

"I don't know."

"What do you mean, you don't know? I thought when people were deployed, they were given a specific timeframe."

"Most people are. We're deployed where and when needed."

Nora frowned. "What are you? Some kind of special forces team?"

His lips pressed together. "Can't say."

She sat back. He was some kind of Special Forces. "Army, right?"

He nodded.

That would make him Delta Force. The elite of the elite. A very skilled soldier who undertook incredibly dangerous missions. She gulped and stopped herself from reaching across the table to take his hand. "Well, I hope all goes well while you and your team are here."

"Thanks."

A man hurried across the chow hall wearing shorts and an Army T-shirt. He headed directly toward their table.

Nora didn't recognize him. "Expecting someone?" she asked Rucker, tipping her head toward the man.

Rucker turned, a frown pulling his eyebrows together. "Why the hell's Dash awake?"

Nora frowned. "Dash? Please tell me that's his callsign, not his real name."

Rucker laughed. "It should be his real name. He's first into the fight, and he's fast." Rucker stood and faced his teammate. "What's up?"

"CO wants us all in the Tactical Operations Center," Dash said. "On the double."

"Guess that's my cue to exit." Rucker turned to Nora. "I enjoyed our talk."

She nodded. "Me, too."

Dash grinned. "Tell you what...I'll stay and finish your conversation while you see what the commander wants."

Rucker hooked Dash's arm twisted it up behind his back, and gave him a shove toward the door. "You heard the CO, he wants all of us." Rucker winked at Nora. "I hope to see you on the volleyball court before you leave."

"Same. Good luck." Nora's gaze followed Rucker's broad shoulders and tight ass out of the chow hall. Too bad she'd only be there another week before she shipped out. She would've enjoyed more volleyball and coffee with the Delta Force operative.

He'd probably be on maneuvers that entire week.

She stacked her tray and coffee cup in the collection area and left the chow hall, heading for the building where she shared her quarters with Beth Drennan, a nurse she'd become friends with during their deployment together.

As close as they were, Nora didn't bring up her conversation with the Delta. With only a week left at the base, she probably wouldn't run into him again. Though she would like to see him again, she prayed he didn't end up in the hospital.

CHAPTER 2

"DAWG, ARE YOU IN POSITION?" Rucker spoke softly into his mic. He hunkered low at the corner of a mud and stick Afghan building, looking across at their target structure, which was less than twenty yards away. He had yet to engage his night vision goggles. The light from the stars shining brightly above illuminated the little village and cast sufficient shadows to hide the Deltas.

A couple of Taliban guards leaned against the structure, half asleep, their AK-47 rifles pointed at the ground.

Ryan "Dash" Hayes was in position at the corner of the structure cattycorner from Rucker, ready to leapfrog to the front entrance when Dawg, their best sniper, reported he was in position at the top of one of the buildings overlooking their location.

Dawg would provide cover while they moved in,

breached the building and extracted their mark, a high-ranking member of the Taliban known for his particularly gory torture of captured American troops and his trade in human trafficking of women and little girls.

"Bull?" Rucker prompted.

"In position," Craig "Bull" Bullington responded.

"Any trouble?" Rucker tensed as one guard's head jerked back, and he straightened, raising his weapon, aiming it in the direction of the road leading through the village. The road they'd have to emerge from soon.

"Two guards on the back wall," Bull said. "I took one. Blade got the other."

"One throw," Michael "Blade" Calhoun said. "The guy probably thought it was a bee sting until he bled out in seconds."

"Mac?" Rucker whispered.

"Got your six," Sean McDaniel responded.

"We're ready when you are," John "Tank" Sanders added.

"Got the village entrance covered," Lance Rankin said. "No one's comin' or goin'."

"Got eyes from the sky on you," Dawg reported.

Rucker's gut twisted. Something didn't feel right.

"I'm going in," Dash announced.

About to tell him to hold steady, Rucker couldn't think of a single obvious reason to abort. The village was quiet. Too quiet.

Intelligence sources had identified this residence as the one currently housing Abdul Akund, a field commander who'd been released by Afghan forces and been on the run for over a year, wreaking havoc on whatever town he targeted as anti-Taliban. He'd hidden in the hills for much of the time. Capturing or killing him would help save Afghan and American lives.

Still, Rucker would've liked to question the source himself. The village, the night, the silence unnerved him.

Dash moved, leapfrogging to another corner closer to the guarded home. Rucker and Dawg covered.

If one of the guards happened to spot Dash, the other two Deltas would risk breaking the silence and take them out. Their weapons were outfitted with silencers, needed when infiltrating villages. The last thing they wanted was an entire community to wake and get in the way of them taking out one man.

Collateral damage in the way of women and children was frowned upon by folks higher up the command chain.

None of the Delta operatives liked it when women or children were killed in the course of a mission.

Silence was golden. Sneak in, get the job done and get out without raising an alarm was their goal.

Not every mission worked out that way.

As soon as Dash was in position less than fifteen feet from the guards, Rucker made his move. Dash would cover for him, along with Mac and Tank at his rear.

Clinging to the shadows, he made it to his next position without either guard noticing.

He and Dash waited in position until Tank and Mac moved closer.

When they were all in place, Rucker gave the hand motion for Dash to move in and take the guard closest to him.

Rucker and Dash left the relative safety of the building corners and rushed the sentries in front of the building.

Before the guards could aim their weapons, Rucker and Dash had them neutralized.

Rucker stood to the side and pushed open the door. That feeling that something wasn't right returned in full force.

"Ready?" Dash said beside him.

Rucker nodded, lowered his night vision goggles over his eyes and entered the building, his rifle leading the way, his finger resting on the trigger guard.

The door opened into a living area. The space was empty but for a rug and some pillows. At the other end of the room was a hallway, leading into the back of the building.

Dash took point, leading the way down the hallway. Rucker followed.

"I don't like this," Rucker whispered into his mic.

Dash didn't slow. As he approached the first doorway off the hall, he pushed it open.

Rucker opened the one across from it.

"Empty," Dash reported.

"Same," Rucker echoed.

Dash moved toward the end of the corridor.

Rucker peered around him, searching for tripwires near the floor.

As Dash reached out to touch the wooden door, Rucker glanced over his buddy's shoulder at something that didn't look right against the wood.

"Wait," Rucker called out.

Too late, Dash's hand pushed the door in, and his helmet touched the trip wire just above eye-level. Rucker reached out, grabbed Dash by the back of his bulletproof vest and yanked him backward.

An explosion slammed the door into Dash, and Dash into Rucker, knocking them and half the building down.

Shouts sounded, gunfire ripped the air and dust fogged Rucker's vision.

With Dash's weight and the rubble of the building crushing him, Rucker could barely move, much less breathe.

"Dash," he wheezed and bucked beneath his burden.

Dash moaned.

His head ringing from the concussion, Rucker rocked right then left. When he tipped left, Dash rolled slightly.

Pushing hard with his right hand, Rucker tipped left again, and Dash rolled off him.

His legs still trapped beneath Dash, Rucker dragged himself across broken, hand-shaped bricks and debris until he freed his feet. He pushed to his hands and knees, rolled Dash onto his back and shook him gently. "Dash."

Dash moaned and went limp, his head lolling.

With gunfire going off around him, Rucker had no choice but to stand. In a fog of dust and debris, his night-vision goggles were useless. He pushed them up on his helmet, grabbed Dash's arm and bent, hauling him up and over his shoulder in a firefighter's carry.

Still shaken and dizzy from the explosion, Rucker stumbled across broken bricks, crumbled walls and debris, hoping he was headed away from the gunfire. When he finally cleared the building and his feet found the relative smoothness of the dirt street, he picked up the pace.

He'd lost communication with his team, and he probably couldn't have heard them anyway. Not with the way his ears were ringing.

A figure loomed out of the fog of dust.

With his hands full of Dash and his rifle on a sling

over his shoulder, he didn't have time to drop his load and aim.

The figure surged toward him, a rifle leading the charge.

"Rucker?" Mac's voice sounded like it came from the inside of a very deep well.

"Mac?" Relieved, Rucker shook his head in an attempt to clear the dizziness.

Mac jerked his head to the side. "Head out of the village. I've got your six. Tank will cover you along the way."

His head rattled and his strength questionable, Rucker trudged on through the village streets, retracing what he hoped had been his path in. When he reached the last building, he peered out into the night. A chopper hovered fifty yards away.

Though his head swam and his knees threatened to buckle, Rucker lurched forward.

Out of the shadows, Tank emerged. "Let me get one side," he said, through the ringing in Rucker's ear.

Tank helped bring Dash off Rucker's shoulder without jolting him too much. Then he draped one of the injured man's arms over his shoulder. Rucker draped the other over his. They started forward, Dash's feet dragging in the dirt.

Behind them, gunfire popped and cracked in the air.

Rucker couldn't look back. To turn his head

would make him dizzier and stumble. They had to get Dash to the helicopter.

Halfway across the open ground, Rucker felt his strength waning. He refused to give up. Had the situation been reversed, Dash would've done everything in his power to get his friend out of danger. Rucker could do no less, no matter how depleted and banged up he felt.

When he thought he couldn't take another step, Lance Rankin ran up alongside him. "Let me," he yelled over the thumping sound of the chopper blades.

Rucker backed out from under Dash's arm as Lance slid beneath. Between Lance and Tank, they had Dash on the helicopter and laid out on the floor. Immediately, Tank bent over him, checked his breathing and shined a penlight into his eyes.

Relieved of his burden, Rucker turned back toward the village. "I'll go help the others."

Lance grabbed his arm. "You're not going anywhere but onto this helicopter. I'll go help the others. You stay with Dash." He didn't wait for Rucker's response, but gripped his rifle and ran back toward the village.

Rucker looked from Dash's inert form to the village and back, too disoriented to form a clear thought.

"Help me get this man covered," Tank barked. He

tossed a thin thermal blanket toward Rucker. "He's going into shock."

Rucker took the square packet from Tank and unfolded the blanket. Then he climbed into the back of the helicopter, leaned over Dash and spread out the blanket.

As he bent, his head swam, and his vision blurred.

"Sit, Rucker," Tank commanded.

Too woozy to argue, Rucker sat in one of the seats and pinched the bridge of his nose. He had to clear the fog, or he was of no use to anyone. At the very least, he could cover any of his team running toward the helicopter. If he couldn't see straight, he risked shooting one of his brothers.

He watched the cluster of mud and stick buildings that comprised the village, praying for the safe exit of the other operatives. Until they were all safe on board the helicopter, he couldn't rest easy.

As he replayed their entry into the target location, he came to one conclusion. They'd been set up. The intel had been planted in order for the Taliban to surprise them in an attempt to take out as many of the Delta Force operatives as they could. Had they used more explosives, the blast could've killed everyone around. Hopefully, the protective gear Dash wore was enough to keep him alive, even if he was unconscious.

Silhouettes emerged from the shadowy edges of the village, heading for the helicopter at a full run.

Rucker raised his rifle and aimed at the one closest to them.

The man closest to him raised his hands.

Tank reached out and pushed the barrel of Rucker's weapon toward the ground. "They're ours," he shouted.

Rucker nodded and counted as the rest of his team raced across the open clearing and leaped into the helicopter. Bull, Blade, Lance and Mac rushed toward him. At the back of the pack, and nearest to the buildings, Mac turned and dropped to one knee, his rifle raised and aimed at the village.

Rucker drew in a breath and held it, willing his head to clear, his gaze glued to the village. They were still missing one of their team members. He thought hard through the fuzziness.

Dawg. Their sniper positioned on the top of one of the buildings had yet to appear.

A figure detached itself from the shadows and raced in a zigzagging motion toward the chopper.

Mac laid down a steady stream of gunfire to the side of Dawg, shooting at the buildings and the enemy combatants popping up on the rooftops.

Lance ran back to a position parallel with Mac and covered Dawg's other side, keeping the men on top of the building down.

Dawg ran past Mac and Lance and leaped into the chopper, and then turned and provided cover as Lance and Mac made it back.

As the Black Hawk lifted off the ground and flew away from the village, Rucker buckled his safety harness around him.

Only when they were out of gun and mortar range did Rucker let go of the breath he'd been holding. Not only did he let go of the air he'd held in his lungs, he released his hold on consciousness and slipped into the haze that had been creeping in on him since the explosion.

The flight back to their base of operations seemed to pass in a flash. The next thing Rucker remembered was the soft jolt of the helicopter touching down. He lifted his head and blinked his eyes. As soon as he recognized where he was, his attention swung to Dash.

The pilot shut down the engine, and the rotor blades slowed.

"How is he?" Rucker asked Tank.

Tank nodded. "Still breathing, and no major bleeding on the outside. But he's still out."

An ambulance truck pulled up beside the landing pad. Medics hopped out, pulled a stretcher from the rear and carried it to the chopper.

Lance, Mac, Bull, Dawg, Blade and Tank got out and stood to the side as they unloaded Dash from the chopper onto the stretcher and carried him to the ambulance.

"I'm riding with him." Rucker fumbled with the buckles, finally managing to release them. When he got out of the helicopter, his legs felt like rubber. If not for Tank standing beside him, he'd have ended up flat on his face in the dirt.

Tank looped his arm over his shoulder and walked him to the ambulance. "Have the doc look you over while you're at it," he said.

Rucker was more interested in Dash's outcome, not his own. "You'll debrief the CO?"

Tank nodded. "He'll want to talk to you since you were in the building when it exploded."

Rucker pinched the bridge of his nose. "Send him by the medical facility. I'll tell him what I know. And I want to know where the hell they got the intel. That bastard led us into a trap."

Tank's lips pressed into a thin line. "Never was so happy to see your ugly face coming out of that cloud of smoke and dust."

"Shouldn't have happened. Dash shouldn't have taken the hit."

"Agreed." Tank took Rucker's rifle and handgun. "I'll stow these in the armory until you and Dash are back at the unit." He helped Rucker into the back of the ambulance onto a bench seat beside the medic establishing an IV in Dash's arm. He caught the medic's attention. "Watch this one, too." He tipped his head toward Rucker. "He was out on the ride back."

"Gotcha," the medic said. He finished with the IV, checked Dash's vitals and turned to Rucker. "How many fingers do you see?" He held up two.

"Two." Rucker frowned. "I'm fine. Take care of my buddy."

"I've done what I can for the moment. He's breathing, he's not bleeding profusely and his heart's beating steadily."

"But he's still out cold."

"The docs will take it from here." The medic flashed a light into Rucker's eyes.

Rucker grabbed the man's wrist. "I'm fine," he said through gritted teeth.

The medic raised an eyebrow and stared at Rucker's hand on his wrist.

Rucker released the man.

"Look, we're here to make sure you guys are fit to fight. I'll look out for your buddy, just don't take whatever you went through out on me." He tipped his head. "Deal?"

Rucker nodded and immediately regretted it. Pain knifed through his temple. He winced before he could stop himself.

"When you get to the treatment facility you should at least let a doc check you out. You look like you've been through hell."

"Fine." Rucker stared out the back as the ambulance door closed. His team stood staring back.

He wished it had been him taking the lead on that door instead of Dash. Dash had family back in the States. A sister who cared about him. Rucker had no one to go home to. No one who would miss him if he were to die. He should have taken point.

What killed him was that he'd had that feeling something wasn't right. That instinct had saved him on multiple occasions. Why had he chosen this mission to ignore it?

The ambulance stopped outside the medical care facility where the Forward Surgical Team was located. As soon as the Army ambulance came to a halt, the medic jumped out.

Rucker dropped to the ground and leaned against the side of the vehicle while they unloaded Dash. He followed his friend into the facility, giving the medics enough space to do their job.

A sturdy nurse stepped in front of Rucker, physically blocking his path. "I'm sorry, but you can't go with your friend into the examination room." She waved a hand toward another door. "If you'll come with me, I'll have a doctor check your wounds."

"I don't need a doctor," Rucker said.

The woman crossed her arms over her chest. "*You* might not, but your wounds might."

Rucker tilted his head toward his friend on the stretcher disappearing through the door. "That's my buddy. I'm with him until he leaves this facility."

"When they get him settled, I'll take you to him. In the meantime, you're a walking germ bath, and you have wounds that could fester if not cleaned." She cocked an eyebrow. "You want to take infection in to your friend?"

Rucker frowned. "Of course not."

"Then I suggest you make use of our shower facility. I'll find some scrubs for you to wear. By the time you're done, the doctor will have had a chance to look over your friend and will have time to look over your wounds."

Rucker let the woman lead him through another door and into a shower facility.

"Leave your clothes outside the door. I'll have a member of the staff bag them for you to take with you when you leave," she said.

Rucker nodded, stepped through the door and started stripping out of his flack vest, shirt jacket and T-shirt. With every layer, he shed fine powdery dust on the floor.

When he stood naked, he pinched the bridge of his nose, fighting back the pain throbbing in his head. It was nothing compared to what Dash was going through. He'd taken the hit, his body shielding Rucker's.

Dash was his friend. The brother he'd never had growing up. Dash gave him hell like only brothers did. But when the shit hit the fan, he was there for Rucker, and Rucker should've been there for him. He should've been the one to open that door, to trigger that bomb.

Drawing in a deep, steadying breath, he turned

the knob on the faucet and stepped beneath the cool spray. The water created streaks of mud that slid down his body to pool at his feet and slip down the drain.

He squirted soap into his hands and scrubbed his hair, face and body, not wanting to bring dirt and germs into the hospital environment. Dash's open wounds needed a sterile environment to heal.

Making quick, efficient work of cleaning his body, he rinsed thoroughly then reached for the towel folded neatly on a stand beside the shower and dried himself. While he'd been in the shower, someone had slipped a set of scrubs through the door onto a chair. The faded green fabric felt soft against his skin. He slipped into the garment, wishing he had his own shorts and a T-shirt, but he didn't want to take the time to go back to his quarters to retrieve clothes. He'd been away too long as it was.

Whoever had left the scrubs had left a large trash bag. Rucker quickly stuffed all his clothes into the bag and tied it. Then he slung it over his shoulder and emerged from the shower unit.

The nurse who'd shown him to the shower unit appeared. With a curt nod, she said, "Follow me."

She led him through the maze of hallways, past small rooms to one at the end. It was empty.

He turned to the nurse. "Where's Dash?"

"He's getting an MRI to check for bleeding on the

brain. When he's done, we'll bring him to this room. You can wait for him here."

He nodded. "Thank you."

"In the meantime, I have a doctor headed your way. I suggest you cooperate and let him check you out." The nurse didn't wait for Rucker's argument. She spun on her heels and left the room.

A tall, thin man, wearing desert camouflage and a stethoscope draped around his neck, entered the room. "The nurse says you and your buddy were hit by an explosion."

"Yes, sir," Rucker said. "The door Dash was about to open hit him full in the chest and knocked us both backward."

"That door probably saved his life. That and his flack vest," the doc said. He shined a light into Rucker's eyes. "Head hurt?"

Rucker shrugged. "A little."

"Were you unconscious at any time since the explosion?"

"No, sir."

"You plan on staying with Hayes tonight?"

Rucker stiffened. "Yes, sir. Is there a problem with that?"

"Not at all." The doctor checked the scrapes and cuts on his arm. "That way we can keep an eye on both of you." He nodded toward Rucker's arms "I'll have the nurse bandage some of those. Can't have you getting a staph infection while in our facility."

"Doc, is Dash going to be all right?"

The man captured Rucker's gaze. "We won't know until he wakes up. Head injuries can be tricky. We didn't see any bleeding on the brain, but that doesn't mean there wasn't any. Until he wakes up, we're shooting in the dark."

"I'll be here all night," Rucker said.

"Good. Sometimes, all it takes is a familiar voice to bring a patient back to consciousness."

Rucker dropped into the chair against the wall and waited.

The nurse who'd shown him to the room returned with bandages and antibacterial gel. She had the lacerations on his arms dressed in a few short minutes.

"Thank you," he murmured as she gathered her supplies and left.

It wasn't long before they wheeled Dash into the room. He lay against crisp white sheets, his eyes closed, an IV drip feeding fluids into his arm. Some of the dirt had been washed away from his face. The cuts had been bandaged, and he looked like he was just sleeping.

Rucker stood over his bed for a long time.

"Dude, you better be all right. The team needs you." He snorted softly. "Though we might have to rethink your being point man. Not sure how many hits you can take and keep on ticking."

Dash lay still, not moving or twitching at all.

Rucker stared at his chest to make sure he was still breathing. He wasn't on oxygen, and though he was hooked up to a heart monitor, the steady beep of the machine was reassuring. Still, they'd have to wait until he was awake to know the extent of the damage.

Until then, Rucker would be there for him. He settled in the chair beside the bed. His body felt like it had been put through a rock tumbler. He had bruises and cuts all over, and his head felt like someone was pounding it like a bass drum. Ignoring the pain, he propped his elbow on the chair's arm and leaned his cheek on his palm.

He'd sleep with one eye open. Any movement on Dash's part would bring him awake.

Okay, so maybe he would close both eyes. The ringing in his ears from the explosion had dissipated. He'd hear Dash if he moved or moaned.

Rucker would be there for Dash when he woke. That's what friends were for. Dash would do the same for him.

Not an overly religious man, Rucker found himself praying for his brother in arms. "Any bit of help you can give him would be appreciated."

CHAPTER 3

"Nora," a voice whispered loudly enough it woke her from a dead sleep.

"What?" She sat up straight in her cot and rubbed the sleep from her eyes. "Am I late for work?" She squinted at Beth, the nurse she shared quarters with.

Beth shook her head. "No, but I thought you'd want to know that the cute soldier you've been flirting with is in the medical facility. You might want to look your best when you go on duty."

Nora's heart skipped several beats. "Why is he in the medical facility?"

"They brought one of his teammates in unconscious. They were both caught in an explosion."

Nora blinked. All vestiges of sleep flew out of her head. "Is Rucker—Sergeant Sloan—okay?"

"Seemed to be, though it took someone of higher rank to make him agree to being treated."

"Damned stubborn ass." Nora threw back the sheet and swung her legs over the side of the cot. "How's his teammate?"

"External injuries appear minor, but he hasn't regained consciousness."

A frown pulled at Nora's forehead.

"I didn't mean for you to go in early. I'm sure he'll be there when you go on shift," Beth said.

"I needed to get up anyway. I'm on midnight to eight." She frowned at her roommate. "How did you know I was talking to Sergeant Sloan?"

Beth rolled her eyes. "It's a small base with an active grapevine."

"Inga saw us in the chow hall?" Nora asked.

"Who else?" Beth smiled. "And I'm glad she shared. How am I supposed to know what my room-mate is up to if she doesn't share all the juicy details?"

"Sorry. I didn't think anything of it. He filled a space on the volleyball court, and we had coffee together. Nothing more."

"Uh huh," Beth said with a sly side-eye look.

"Seriously." Nora shoved her feet into her boots and pulled the laces taut. "I'm out of here in a week. Not to mention, he's enlisted. I'm an officer. Not only is fraternization taboo between officers and enlisted, it'll get you court-martialed if you engage in it while deployed."

Beth crossed her arms over her chest. "That doesn't stop you from thinking about it, does it?"

Nora straightened and grimaced. "Not in the least. Why does he have to be so damned..." she held her hands out to the width of Rucker's shoulders, "...sexy?"

"Ha! I knew it. You finally found someone to drool over."

"For what it's worth. Hello," she said, "I'm leaving in a week. And I'm not going to act on my urges."

"But you do have urges."

"Of course, I do."

"Thank God," Beth said. "I thought you were going to enter a convent after your tour of duty."

Nora slipped her arms into her uniform jacket and headed for the door of their quarters, buttoning as she went. "I'm not a nun. He's sexy but completely off limits."

"And that's why you're running out the door to get to him." Beth's laugh followed her from the building.

As she ran toward the medical facility, Nora completed buttoning her jacket, twisted her hair into a tight bun at the base of her skull and secured it in place with the pins from her pocket. Then she jammed her hat onto her head and ran the rest of the way through the dimly lit streets of the base. When she arrived at the facility, she slowed, brought her breathing under control and walked in.

"Lieutenant Michaels, you're here early for your

shift." The female specialist at the front desk smiled as she entered.

"I heard you actually had some patients and thought you might need an extra hand."

"We do. I think there was only one badly injured and one with minor lacerations. But you can ask Captain Williams. Doctor Eddy was here a while ago, but he's gone to his quarters for the night."

"I'll check with Captain Williams." Nora wandered through to where the nurses entered data into the computer system.

Captain Inga Williams sat at her desk, entering information into a patient's chart. Having joined the Army in her thirties, she was closing in on forty, a little stout, her brown hair lightly salted with early gray. She looked and acted stern, but Nora knew it was all an act. She had a big heart and gave each patient the attention they needed.

Nora had seen her hold a soldier's hand who'd been severely injured in a helicopter crash. He'd been scared and couldn't see because of burns to his face. She'd sat beside his bed throughout the night, even after her shift had ended.

"You're early," she said in her blunt, direct way.

"Thought you might need a hand. Heard you had some patients come in while I was sleeping."

"We did. Your guy seems to be holding his own. Practically had to threaten him to get him to let us treat his wounds," she said, pursing her lips in disapproval.

"Why does everyone seem to think he's my guy? We played volleyball and drank coffee. Nothing else."

The captain arched an eyebrow. "You haven't sat alone with a male since you came here, much less laughed and talked for a good half hour with one. I'd say you might like him a little."

"I barely know him."

"Sometimes, not knowing a man is better than knowing too much about him. The mystery is what attracts us."

Nora stared at Captain Williams. She'd never talked on such a personal level before, offering emotional advice to Nora.

The older nurse frowned. "What? You think I've never been in love? That I've always been an old soul with salt and pepper gray hair?" She shook her head. "I never told you that I married my high school sweetheart right after graduation. We were together for eight years before he died in an automobile accident."

Nora's heart constricted. "I didn't know. I'm so sorry."

The captain shrugged. "It's been years, but I still miss him. He got me like no one else ever has. He thought I was beautiful, even when my hair started turning gray in my twenties." Her lips turned up in a wistful smile as she stared at the wall in front of her.

Then her smile faded, and she looked up at Nora. "The point is, I know what it's like to fall in love."

"I'm not in love," Nora insisted. "We only had coffee in a crowded mess hall."

"And yet, you're here as soon as you heard he was." Captain Williams raised her eyebrows for a second, and then hooked her thumb over her shoulder. "He's in the last room on the right with his friend who was hit full on by an explosion. The friend has been unconscious since impact."

Nora frowned. "Any bleeding on the brain?"

"The MRI didn't show any. We won't know the complete extent of the injuries until the man wakes up. Sergeant Sloan insisted on staying with him until that event occurs."

"Think they need anything?" Nora asked.

"Won't know until you ask." Captain Williams jerked her head to the side. "Go on. And take a blanket and a pillow. Sloan is sitting in a very hard chair. The least we can do is offer him some comfort. He was in that same explosion."

"And he wasn't injured as badly?"

"Apparently, his friend stood between him and the explosive device. He was knocked down and received a few shrapnel wounds and some bruises, but all in all, he's been released for duty."

"Are you still coming with me to the orphanage tomorrow?" Nora asked.

Captain Williams shook her head. "The doctor

wants me to stay and do an inventory of our supplies. You'll need to reschedule the visit."

"I can do it on my own. We're just performing inoculations and doing a quick exam, right?"

"There are thirty little ones in that place. It could take you all day by yourself." The older nurse shook her head. "I'd rather you waited."

"They've been looking forward to our visit for a while now." Nora sighed. "I really don't mind putting in the extra time."

"You'll miss out on your usual sleep."

"I can sleep when I get back to the States," Nora said. "This will be my last chance to see the children."

Captain Williams tapped her chin with the pen in her hand. "I haven't canceled the armed escort."

"See? You knew I'd want to go, no matter what."

"Maybe you can get Lieutenant Drennan to go with you."

"I'll ask." She knew Beth had plans for the next day. Either way, she was going. She wanted to say goodbye to the children. If she could, she'd take them all home with her and raise them as her own, especially little Taara, the two-year-old, dark-haired, dark-eyed toddler. She deserved a better life than what she'd have.

Nora grabbed a blanket and pillow from one of the laundry supply cabinets and hurried down the hallway to the last room, pushing gently against the swinging door to enter.

A man lay against the stark white sheets, his face bruised, his hair matted with debris and blood. The steady beep of the heart monitor reassured her that he was still alive, and his heart was beating with a healthy rhythm.

In the chair on the other side of him sat the man who'd been on her mind over the past thirty-six hours. She hadn't seen him since they'd talked in the chow hall over coffee. She'd slept during the day and had assumed he was out on a mission the past couple of nights. The mission must not have ended quite as they'd had planned.

Presently, he leaned back against the wall, his head tipped at an uncomfortable angle.

The hospital kept the rooms cool. If he'd been hurt in the explosion, he could go into shock. A blanket was a medical necessity in such a situation.

She crossed the floor, pulled the sheet and blanket up around the patient, the man who'd interrupted their coffee two mornings ago. Dash. By the cuts and bruises on his face, the man had taken a beating. She hoped he didn't have any internal damage or a traumatic brain injury.

He must be a pretty close friend for Rucker to sit by his bed when he could be sleeping in his own cot.

Nora's heart swelled. Not only was Rucker broad-shouldered and sexy, he was also loyal and a good friend, caring for one in his time of need.

Nora had found that men who fought together developed a strong bond between each other.

Rucker and Dash must have been through a lot together.

She draped the blanket over his lap and leaned over to tuck the pillow behind him, lifting his head gently.

When she settled his head back on the pillow, his hand snagged her wrist.

She looked down to discover his eyes were open and staring up into hers.

He pulled on her wrist, bringing her closer.

"Do you need something else?" she whispered.

"Yes, this." He leaned up and captured her lips with his in a tender kiss.

She should've stepped back and slapped his face, but the truth was, she liked his kiss and found herself wanting more.

Then she remembered where she was, and that she could get into big trouble if anyone saw them kissing. Nora jerked upright and stepped back. "You shouldn't have done that." She touched her fingers to her tingling mouth.

"I thought I was dreaming that an angel was kissing me. It only felt right to kiss her back."

"Still, it's against all the rules," she said, her voice barely a whisper.

A single cocky brow rose on his forehead. "Do you always follow the rules?"

She did. But why did he make it sound like a character flaw?

Nora squared her shoulders. She liked structure and rules. They made her life less...messy. "Are you all right?" she asked lifting her chin.

"I am now," he said with a slow, sexy smile.

"I mean, do you have any injuries bothering you at this time?" she asked, trying to make her tone sound all business. Instead, it came out breathy and gravelly all at once.

Shit. She was so turned on, she could barely breathe. What was wrong with her? He was enlisted. She was an officer.

He must have sensed her distress because he changed the subject and nodded toward his buddy. "Is Dash going to be all right? He hasn't come to since the blast."

"Only time will tell," she said, smoothing a loose hair back from her face. "We'll know more when he wakes."

"I hope that's soon." Rucker scrubbed a hand across his rugged face and the stubble growing on his chin.

That shadow had been rough against her skin when he'd kissed her. She wondered what it would feel like skimming across her naked body.

Again, she had to shake herself out of the thoughts she was having toward her patient.

Then again, he wasn't technically her patient. He was a concerned friend of the patient.

And enlisted.

And they were both deployed to a war zone.

Two words echoed in her mind.

Off limits.

"I'm glad you came."

"I work here," she reminded him.

"Not until midnight."

Why did everyone have to point out that she was early? She raised her hands. "Can't a dedicated nurse show up early for her shift, without everyone suspecting an ulterior motive?"

His lips twitched, and then spread into smile. "Did you have an ulterior motive?"

Nora frowned.

His voice lowered into a sexy whisper. "Was it me?"

She lifted her chin and stared down her nose at him. "You have an inflated opinion of yourself, don't you?"

He shrugged. "It's part of the job. If you don't think you're good, you aren't. And you die." His smile faded as he stared at his friend. "Hear that, Dash? You're good, and you know it. Therefore, you can't die. Get your lazy ass out of that bed and back to work."

Nora watched as a slight frown tugged at Dash's forehead. Had he heard his friend badmouth him?

"That's right," Rucker said. "I called you lazy. Whatcha gonna do about it?"

Half expecting Dash to get out of the bed and slam a fist into his friend's face, Nora was more surprised that he didn't. She shined a pen light into his eye. The pupil constricted.

"Anyone home?" Rucker asked.

"He's still out, but there was a reaction to the light. He might surface anytime, or it might be a while."

Rucker nodded. "Time will tell. God, I'm tired of hearing that. I want to shake Dash awake and walk out of the medical facility with him. I hate everything about being near a hospital bed." He frowned as he stared up at her. "Except one pretty nurse."

She laughed. "I'm glad you made that distinction." Her lips thinned. "Sometimes, I hate my job. But I don't hate the facility. It can be where miracles happen."

"Or not," Rucker gritted out.

"Your friend is breathing, and his heartbeat is regular. He's got more going for him than a lot of soldiers do who come through here."

Rucker scrubbed his hand over his face again and sighed. "I know. I'm just not a very patient man. When I set out to do something, I like to get it done immediately." He waved a hand at Dash. "This trying my patience. Not only is he taking forever to wake up, I don't have the patience to wait for that to happen."

"Then why are you here, sitting by Dash's bedside?"

His frown deepened into a fierce glare. "He's my friend. And he, by God, better live and get back to the team."

The man on the bed stirred.

Rucker was out of his chair in a second. "Dash? You hear me?"

"Do you ever shut up?" Dash said, his voice coming out as croak.

Rucker's face split in a grin. "Dude, next time you're too lazy to walk your own ass out of a situation, let me know so I can have Tank or Bull there to carry you out. Have you been packing away the candy bars?"

"Every chance I get," Dash said with a tired smile. "What happened? Where am I? Who's the angel over your shoulder?"

"Nothing for you to see, Dash," Rucker said, moving to block his view of the nurse.

Nora elbowed him aside. "Sergeant Hayes, you're in a medical facility."

"How long have I been out?"

"Long enough for me to haul your ass out of that village, toss you onto a helicopter and catch a few Zs while you slept," Rucker recounted. "About five hours."

"Damn—I mean, dang." He gave Nora a weak grimace then lifted his arms and legs. "Whew. The gang's all here."

"Not funny," Rucker said. "That blast could've done more damage than knocking you out. A good thing that door was thick enough to shield you from the bulk of the shrapnel or you would have been Swiss cheese."

"Lucky me." He groaned. "Not feeling very lucky right now."

"What hurts?" Nora asked.

"Would be easier to ask what doesn't hurt," Dash said.

"I'll get the doctor in to check you over now that you're awake. He'll want to ask you a few questions."

"Seeing as I'm a captive audience," Dash said, "and the bed is softer than the one in my quarters, I guess I could stay the night."

"Glad you're back, man," Rucker said.

"Thanks for getting me out of there." Dash frowned. "When my head's a little clearer, you'll have to tell me what happened."

"Will do."

Nora left the room and hurried back to Captain Williams. "Dash—Sergeant Hayes—is awake."

The captain nodded. "I'll have the doctor notified." She raised her eyebrows. "Find your guy?"

Nora rolled her eyes. "He's not my guy."

"Yeah. Then why are your cheeks turning red?"

"Look, I'm not going to do anything that will jeopardize my commission."

"He's not in your chain of command," Captain Williams said.

Nora stared at her like she'd lost her mind. "You're not condoning a fling, are you?"

The captain sighed. "No. Legally, I can't. It's against all the rules. But I am a romantic at heart. There have to be some bright spots in this godforsaken war."

"Well, it's not going to be me falling for a man who is clearly forbidden," Nora said.

Captain Williams's lips quirked, and she tilted her head toward the door behind Nora. "Can I help you with something?" she said to someone standing behind Nora.

Nora's cheeks burned. She didn't have to turn around to know Rucker was standing behind her. Her skin tingled, and her pulse picked up. Even if she hadn't seen the smirk on her supervisor's face, she'd have known it was him.

Nora spun to face Rucker. "How much of that conversation did you overhear?"

He held up his hands. "I heard nothing."

She narrowed her eyes and stared at his wide-eyed, innocent expression. "None of it?"

Rucker lifted one shoulder. "I might have heard the word 'forbidden'. They say the best tasting fruit is always forbidden." He winked and smiled at the captain. "Am I right?"

"Completely," the older nurse said. "Are you headed to your quarters now that your friend is awake?"

"No, actually, he's asking for food." Rucker grinned. "Dash loves his chow."

"He must be feeling much better," Nora said. "I can run to the chow hall and see what I can rustle up," Nora offered. "My shift doesn't officially start for another fifteen minutes."

"Good. While you're getting him something to eat, I'll check on the patient and assist the doctor when he arrives," Captain Williams said. "No need for you to stay," she said to Rucker.

"Then I'll help Lieutenant Michaels find food. I could use some myself." Rucker held open the door for Nora. "After you."

She could've told him she didn't need help. But then, he'd probably go with her anyway.

The man was making it really hard for Nora to keep her distance. Especially when she really didn't want to.

CHAPTER 4

RUCKER HAD BEEN SO relieved that Dash was finally awake and well enough to ask for food that he could have kissed Nora all over again.

However, he understood her reticence. The rules were clear. Fraternization was strictly forbidden and punishable according to the Uniform Code of Military Justice.

For kissing her, she could have him up on charges. He could be kicked out of the military.

He cast a glance in her direction as they walked in the darkness toward the chow hall.

Yeah, he could get kicked out, but he'd do it all over again. Her lips had been as soft as he'd imagined, and she hadn't protested. If he wasn't mistaken, she'd returned the kiss, if ever so lightly. He could blame it all on waking from a dream, but that would only be half true. He hadn't been asleep, though he had been dreaming of her ever since he'd met her.

"Thanks for coming when you heard Dash was hurt."

She shrugged. "I'd rather have too many hands on deck than be short-handed for a mass casualty event." She smiled. "Thankfully, it wasn't. What happened out there? Or can't you talk about it?"

"I can't give specifics. All I know is I saw the trip-wire about the time Dash hit it. He was opening a door. That door probably saved his life. I was right behind him. Between the door and Dash, they saved my life."

"I'm glad," she said simply.

They continued walking in silence.

"So, you're leaving in a few days. Any chance you'll be playing volleyball again before then?" Rucker asked. He'd do anything to spend time with her, even if he had to share it with others.

"I doubt it," she spoke softly in the night. "I'm heading out to the local orphanage tomorrow to deliver vaccinations for the children."

Rucker frowned. "How are you getting there?"

"We usually have a driver take us, and two additional vehicles with armed soldiers as escorts."

He was sure that his commander had something on the slate for his team the next day but considering that last night's mission had ended in near disaster, he suspected they wouldn't be going out the following day. A plan formed. He'd make certain he was on the detail taking Nora to the orphanage, even if he had to give up some much-needed rest to do it. He'd gone days without sleep before. He could do it again.

Something about her made him want to spend more time with her. Maybe it was her long, lithe form, or the savage way she'd spiked a volleyball. He would bet his paycheck that she was as passionate in bed as she was on the volleyball court.

Too bad he wouldn't find out.

Nora was on her way home soon.

As well, he had no idea how long the team would be in Afghanistan. Probably until they captured Abdul Akund. Since their intelligence had been faulty to the point of almost fatal, it was now a matter of pride and payback to find the bastard and the people who'd set them up to take the fall. Dash could've been killed in that explosion.

They entered the chow hall together. The lights were brightly lit inside for the personnel working the night shift. Though food choices weren't as varied, they were able to find ham and bread for ham sandwiches.

Loading up a tray full of food, they headed back to the medical facility, passed Nurse Williams' empty office and continued down the hallway to Dash's room.

The nurse and doctor were leaving as they approached.

"Is he going to live?" Rucker asked.

"If he's feeling this good in the morning, I'll sign his release. A couple days light duty should be sufficient," the doctor said.

Captain Williams nodded. "He's lucky he got off that lightly." She eyed the tray. "Good thing you came with the food. He's starting to get irritable."

Rucker chuckled. "That's how he operates. I keep a granola bar handy when he gets cranky."

"Get that boy some granola bars," the doctor said. "No food restrictions. We didn't see any bleeding on the brain, and other than some bruised ribs and a few lacerations we sewed up, he should be ready for duty in a couple of days."

"Glad to hear it," Rucker said. "Thanks, Doc."

"I'm calling it a night, Lieutenant," Captain William said. "I'll need to go over the charts with you before I leave."

"Coming," Nora said.

"I can feed the beast," Rucker said.

Nora left him to follow the captain to her office. The doctor disappeared through another door, and Rucker pushed through the door into Dash's room.

"Sweet Jesus," Dash said. "I swear I must have a tapeworm. I'm hungry enough to eat everything on that tray and the tray itself."

"You'll have to share. One of these sandwiches is mine."

"Hey, I'm the injured party here. I should be allowed to eat all the sandwiches."

Rucker handed Dash a napkin.

The point man tucked it beneath his chin and held out his hands for the ham sandwich. Once he had it, he sank his teeth into the bread and meat, moaning noisily. "Oh, yeah. Now, we're talking." After he'd consumed the entire sandwich and washed it down with a carton of milk, he sighed, leaned back against the pillow and closed his eyes.

"How do you feel?" Rucker asked.

"Like a truck hit me." He popped his eyes open and looked at Rucker. "Thanks for getting me out."

"Had to," Rucker said. "Says in my contract with the Army, *leave no man behind.*" He laughed. "Besides, I don't want your job as point man. Too risky."

"You think?" Dash pressed his fingers to his temples. "They gave me a painkiller. I hope it kicks in soon."

"It should. What do you want me to tell the CO?"

"What the doctor said. They'll let me loose in the morning. After a day in my quarters, I should be good to return to duty."

Rucker frowned. "That's not what I heard. The good doc said a *couple* of days. Not one day."

"A day here, a day there. I'm fine. Just a headache and a few bruises. Nothing I wouldn't have gotten playing basketball with you dumbasses." He closed his eyes again, a smile pulling at his lips. "Or volleyball. Speaking of which...I can see why you liked playing so much. She's hot. I might have to take up the sport while I'm convalescing."

Rucker set aside his half-eaten sandwich, suddenly not all that hungry. "She ships out in less than a week."

"Plenty of time to get in a game or two," Dash said.

Rucker's fists clenched. "She's not playing between now and her departure."

Dash opened his eyes in narrow slits. "So, you asked." He grinned. "Is she playing hard to get?"

"She's a rule follower."

"Pulled the old fraternization card, did she?" Dash nodded. "I've had women who vowed to be celibate only to give it up when my charm and wit became too much to resist."

Rucker snorted. "Since when have you had a relationship with an officer?"

Dash's smile faded. "It happened. It's over. I'm over it. No one was court-martialed, or I wouldn't be here today licking my wounds."

"I didn't know that." Rucker shook his head.

"Yeah, well, now you do." Dash frowned. "But that's between me, you and the IV bag. Wouldn't want anyone to lose his or her job because of me.

Besides, it would never have worked. We had different goals in life."

"What goals?"

"I wanted someone forever." He shrugged. "She didn't."

"I'm sorry it didn't work out."

"Like I said. It wasn't meant to be."

"And anything between me and the pretty lieutenant isn't meant to be. I don't know why I even think I have a shot at her."

"Because she seems to like you." Dash smirked. "Though what she sees in you beats the hell out of me."

Rucker frowned. "You really think she likes me?"

"I'm lying in a hospital bed with a bazillion holes in me." He raised his eyebrows. "You think I'd lie to you when I feel like I do?"

Rucker studied his friend. "Not unless it involves food. How you eat like you do and aren't nudging the weight limits is beyond me."

"High metabolism, my man. High metabolism." Dash patted his flat belly. "You should try it."

"Shut up." Rucker touched a hand to his own flat abs. "I have to work for mine."

"You're avoiding the subject." Dash brought him back to his dilemma. "What are you going to do about the hot lieutenant?"

"Probably nothing."

"I've never known you to do nothing about a beautiful woman."

"Well, this might be a first."

"Uh-huh." Dash narrowed his eyes. "I can see the gears turning in your head. You're planning something."

Rucker gave his friend his most innocent look. "Don't know what you're talking about. But seeing that you're feeling better and will probably live, I think I'll find a cot and catch some Zs."

Dash snorted. "That's right. Ditch the battle buddy for a pretty nurse. I see where I rank."

When Rucker started to turn, Dash grabbed his wrist.

"You need something before I go?" Rucker asked.

"Yeah." Dash's mouth straightened. "Thanks."

Rucker shrugged. "You'd have done the same." He shrugged free of his friend's grip. "But warn me next time. I'll get Tank or Bull to carry you out."

"Duly noted," Dash said. "Hope things work out for you with the nurse. If they don't, let me know. I wouldn't mind throwing my hat in that ring."

"Bite me." Rucker left the room, a smile tugging at his lips.

Dash was going to be fine. They'd lived to see another day, and he had an idea how he'd get to spend more time with Nora. He'd put that plan in place before he caught a couple hours of shut-eye.

. . .

NORA LEFT her shift an hour late that morning, having spent additional time in the medical facility gathering the supplies they'd need to inoculate up to thirty children for measles, mumps, rubella and polio.

She had several large boxes staged at the front desk with the medical supplies and the donated items she'd received from the States, including children's clothing, toys and shoes.

After returning to her quarters, ducking into the shower tent for a quick rinse and dressing in a fresh uniform, she was ready. She'd had the Army Private First Class at the front desk of the medical unit call for the requisite transport driver and additional armed escort to take her to the orphanage. The base commander encouraged community volunteering. He had children of his own back in the States and liked to see the photographs of the work the doctors and nurses performed on behalf of the local village and its orphans.

Back at the medical facility, she waited for her ride and escort to arrive, checking her watch every two minutes, impatient to get started so that she could see the kids one last time before she packed her few belongings and shipped out. She'd miss them and the people she'd worked with for the past year.

In addition, she had been looking forward to her next assignment, wondering what new adventures it would bring and the people she would meet. Until she'd met a soldier on the volleyball court and had coffee with him. Now, she wished she was staying a little bit longer in Afghanistan.

Nora reminded herself she was an officer. He was enlisted. Beating herself over the head with that information wasn't working. She still wanted to get to know him and spend more time with him. She found him physically irresistible and those impossibly broad shoulders very attractive.

The man exuded confidence like no other individual she'd ever met, and he didn't seem to be afraid to bend or even break a few rules. It gave him a little aura of danger. She found that titillating. It made her hot in places she hadn't been hot in for a long time.

It was just as well she was heading off base for the day, otherwise, she'd get herself into trouble looking for the soldier and drooling over his biceps.

Three vehicles pulled up in front of the medical facility and stopped. The first and last were her escorts. The middle vehicle was a HUMMV. The men in the escort vehicles helped her load the boxes into the back of the HUMMV.

While she supervised the loading, her driver walked off.

Nora frowned. Now, where was he going? They were due to leave as soon as the supplies were in the back of the vehicle.

A moment later, another man, wearing desert camouflage, his helmet pulled down low over his face trotted over to the HUMMV and slipped in behind the steering wheel.

About time, Nora thought.

She thanked the men who would be her escorts and climbed into the front seat of the HUMMV. When she turned to the driver, she gasped. "You!"

Rucker grinned. "Surprise."

Nora frowned. "You're not my driver."

"I am today." He pointed to the vehicle's logbook. "I signed for the vehicle. I'm the driver."

"Do you even know where we're going?"

"I figure I can follow the guy in front of me. He should know."

Her frown deepened.

"Yes, of course, I know. I've studied the maps and have the GPS coordinates as well. If we lose our escorts, we'll still get there."

"Good Lord. We'd better not lose our escorts. It can be dangerous traveling without one."

"Tell me about it," he said with a grin and started the engine.

Nora sat in the passenger seat, twisting her fingers together as Rucker pulled in behind the lead vehicle and drove past the armed guards at the base gate.

"This is a bad idea," she murmured.

"What did you say?" Rucker asked over the roar of the engine.

"Nothing. I hope you're ready to be bored while I take care of the children."

"You can put me to work doing whatever you need me to do."

"How are you with needles?" she asked.

He grinned. "When they're pointed at someone else, I'm fine."

"How are you about children?"

"I think everyone should have two or three."

Her lips twitched. "I mean, do you get along with them? Some people don't even like children."

"I get along fine with children, dogs and even the occasional cat."

"Children aren't animals."

"No, they aren't. Animals are trainable." He winked. "Don't worry. Kids like me."

"You're just so big, I don't want to scare them."

"Scare them? I'm more worried they'll scare me." His eyes flashed with humor. "I have scars from some of my buddy's rug rats."

"Good grief, what were you doing with them?"

"Let's not talk about that. Suffice it to say, an umbrella is not a parachute." He faced forward, his attention on the road leading through the nearby town.

As was typical, the streets were filled with people moving to and from work, the market and their homes.

The three vehicles moved slowly through the

busy streets until they were a couple blocks short of the edge of town where they picked up a little speed.

Rucker gave the lead vehicle a little more distance between them.

A donkey-pulled cart darted from the side of the road, wedging its way between the lead vehicle and the one Rucker was driving.

He slammed on the brakes and swerved right.

Nora pitched forward and to the left, her seatbelt saving her from slamming into the dashboard.

"Hang on," Rucker said. "We might have some trouble." He'd swerved onto a side street to avoid hitting the donkey and his cart.

Nora glanced over her shoulder at the rear escort vehicle.

A man on a scooter swerved toward a merchant's display of tapestry rugs and hand-woven baskets, knocking over a large rack holding a significant number of rugs and baskets. They fell into the street, blocking the rear escort vehicle.

"I don't think this is an accident," Rucker said through gritted teeth as he gunned the accelerator and sent the HUMMV through the narrow side street.

A moment later, a man in the white robes of a native Afghan jumped onto the front hood and pointed a handgun at Nora.

She screamed and raised her arms in front of her face.

Rucker slammed on the brakes in an attempt to lose the attacker.

The man must have anticipated his move, because he hooked his hand into the space between the hood and the windshield holding on tightly. He shouted. "Stop, or I will shoot the woman."

Nora's heart slammed against her ribs, beating so fast she thought it might leap right out of her chest.

"I can't turn left or right with the buildings so close on either side." He punched the accelerator, shooting forward fast and furious and slammed on his brakes again.

The man held fast.

When the vehicle came to a stop again, the man shot a round through the windshield between Nora and Rucker. "The next round goes into the woman."

"Just stop," Nora said, her shoulder hurting from being slung against the seatbelt multiple times. She'd looked over her shoulder. What had been an empty street or alley was now full of people, carts and small children. "I don't want anyone hurt by flying bullets."

"If we stop, we lose any control over the situation," Rucker said.

"I'd rather lose control than take out civilians as collateral damage," she said.

Rucker shook his head. "It's not good."

The man on the hood aimed his pistol at Nora. "Stop now," he yelled.

Two more men appeared beside the HUMMV, aiming rifles at the window.

"Where are our escorts?" Rucker bit out, reaching for his handgun.

"On the other side of those civilians." Nora laid a hand on his arm. "You bring your weapon out, and they'll for sure start shooting."

His lips pressed into a thin line. "I can't let them take you."

"We don't have a choice at this point," she reasoned. "They outnumber us in guns and people."

The man riding on the hood yelled, "Get out."

Rucker shouted back. "I go with the woman."

"No. You get out," the man shouted.

"You'll have to shoot me," Rucker said.

"No," Nora said. "We'll go with you. But we go together," she said, her pulse hammering. She wanted to throw herself in front of Rucker to keep their attackers from putting a bullet through him.

The gunman on Rucker's side pounded on the window. "Give me your gun."

"Do it," Nora said.

Rucker rolled down the window and handed the gun out to the man beside him.

The man tucked it into his belt and reached in to unlock the back door. He climbed in and unlocked the other side. The other gunman got in and scooted over, aiming his rifle at Rucker's head.

"Don't shoot," Nora pleaded.

The man on the hood slid off and climbed in the back seat with the other two. "Drive," he ordered.

"Where?" Rucker asked.

"I will tell you when to turn," he said. "Drive."

Rucker eased forward and out into another cross street, careful not to hit anyone passing in front of him. At the next road, the man who'd been on the hood told him to turn left.

A couple blocks later, he had Rucker turn right and drive through a gate into a walled-in home.

As soon as Rucker pulled to a halt, the man who'd risked his life on the hood of the vehicle leaped out of the HUMMV, yanked open Nora's door and pulled her out.

"Rucker," she called out, fear locking the air in her lungs. She dug in her heels, turned and held out her hand.

Rucker was out of his side of the vehicle and around the front before Nora was taken very far. She didn't make it easy on the man holding her arm.

The two men with the rifles closed in on either side of him.

"I go with her," Rucker called out.

Her captor spoke to his cohorts in Pashto.

They nodded, gripped Rucker's arms and followed Nora and her escort into the building.

Inside, Nora heard a woman moaning in pain.

She wondered if the woman was being tortured, and if they would torture her next. Knowing panic would help no one, she forced herself to remain calm and study the building, searching for an opportunity and avenue for escape.

The man gripping her arm dragged her down a long hallway.

The sound of the woman moaning grew louder.

He stopped in front of a door and knocked.

An older woman, wearing a blue hijab wrapped around her head and neck, opened the door and spoke quickly in the native language.

The man replied and shoved Nora forward. "You will help," he said.

"Help to do what?" Nora asked.

"It has been over a day and the baby has not come. You will help my wife."

The older woman gave her a narrow-eyed look and spoke again to the man.

He barked a command to the woman, and she backed away from the door.

Nora looked past her to a bed where a woman lay, her moans weaker now.

Nora stepped past the woman and crossed to the one lying on the bed, her hands gripping the sheets on either side of her. Her belly rose like a small mountain beneath the covers.

Nora hadn't delivered a baby since clinical rotations during her nurse's training, but she'd studied enough and had helped several OB-GYN doctors during that time. Unbuttoning her jacket, she asked, "Who here speaks English?"

The woman in labor whispered. "I speak a little."

"How close are the contractions?"

"Very close."

"For how long?"

"Since sun went down."

"Last night?" Nora's heart skipped several beats. "Has your water broken?"

The woman shook her head. "Yes."

"How long ago?"

"As the sun came up," the woman said and cried out as another contraction took all her breath.

Nora shrugged out of her jacket, tossing it over a pillow on the floor.

Within minutes, she checked to see if the baby's head had crowned. It had not. Instead, with every contraction, the baby's bottom presented.

She smiled to the woman then went out into the hallway to speak to the man who had kidnapped her. "We have a breech presentation."

"What do you mean? What is this breech?" the man Nora presumed was the woman's husband asked.

"It means, it's not coming out headfirst. If we don't help the baby be born, the baby and the mother could die. You need to get her to a hospital."

The husband shook his head. "That is not possible. You will help." He held the gun up, pointing it at Nora's chest.

"I'm a nurse, not a doctor. She needs a caesarian section to remove the baby from her abdomen."

Again, the husband shook his head. "We cannot. If we go to a hospital, it will be reported. We will be targeted."

Nora exchanged a glance with Rucker who stood behind the husband.

"Let me help her," Rucker urged.

Nora studied the soldier. "Have you ever helped with the birth of a baby?"

He nodded. "Actually, I have, twice. Once in Texas on my way home from training, I came across a vehicle parked on the shoulder with its hazards lights on. A woman was standing beside it, holding her belly. I stopped and helped her deliver her baby in the back seat of the car."

"A breech?" Nora asked. "They're a lot more complicated."

"Not a human breech. But I helped a friend of mine back in Texas deliver a breech calf," Rucker said over the husband's shoulder.

Nora's lips pressed together. She stared at the man who'd brought her there at gunpoint. His forehead was creased in a frown. He was truly worried about his wife and child.

Nora addressed him. "Have you delivered a baby?"

The man shook his head. "This is my first child."

"Let my driver in. He will assist."

"My mother will help," the husband said.

"We will need her as well. Let him in," Nora commanded.

The man spoke to his wife.

She gripped the bedsheets as another excruciating contraction ripped through her. She cried out in Pashto.

The husband stepped aside, allowing Rucker into the room.

He entered, shrugged out of his body armor and jacket and turned to Nora. "Tell me what you need me to do."

"For now, I need both of you to hold her legs while I work to deliver the baby."

Nora turned to the husband. "I need the box of gloves from the back of my vehicle." She gave him a narrow-eyed, scowl. "Touch anything else, and I won't help."

The children in the orphanage had enough strikes against them. She was determined that the vaccinations would arrive. If not that day, then the next.

The husband spun and rushed away from the room. His two armed guards remained, standing outside the room on either side of the door.

Rucker leaned forward and asked, "Have you delivered a breech baby before?"

Nora responded in a tone the mother wouldn't

hear. "No, but I've watched the procedure done. It can be delivered without a C-section."

"Then let's get this done. She's getting weaker."

"Hold her leg," Nora instructed.

Rucker looped an arm around the woman's thigh and held it back. The older woman did the same.

The contraction had helped the woman push the baby's bottom into the birth canal.

Nora captured the mother's attention. "Breathe, don't push. I need to get the legs out first."

The woman nodded, sweat beading across her forehead, her face pale.

Nora drew in a deep breath and let it out slowly, showing the mother how to breathe to let the contraction pass without pushing.

The husband returned with the box of gloves.

Nora pulled on a pair. "You should leave," she told the husband.

"She is my wife," he said, his voice tense, his eyes wide. "You must save her and my child."

"We will do what we can," Nora said. "Breech births are very dangerous for the mother and the baby. She really needs to be in a hospital."

Again, the father shook his head "We cannot."

"Then leave and allow me to work with your wife. I'll do my best." She prayed her best was good enough. If it wasn't good enough, and one or both died, would the father kill her and Rucker?

CHAPTER 5

IF YOU'D ASKED Rucker what he'd be doing a couple days after nearly being blown up during a mission, he would never have guessed he'd be holding a stranger's thigh in an attempt to deliver a breech baby.

What he did was nothing compared to what Nora accomplished in her attempt to save the lives of the mother and her unborn baby.

She worked quickly and efficiently, extricating the baby's legs from the birth canal. Once the legs were free, the baby slipped out up to its neck. Then she fished out the arms.

"This is the tricky part," Nora said quietly so that only Rucker could hear. "If we don't get the baby's head out quickly, it will asphyxiate and die."

Holding the baby's body with one hand, she

guided Rucker's other hand to the woman's belly. "When I say push, bear down hard and keep pushing until I tell you to stop. Got it?"

He frowned. "Got it, but what am I doing?"

"I need you to push the baby's head down through the birth canal while I catch it on the other side. Ready?"

Hell no. He wasn't ready.

Nora didn't give him time to think about it. "Push," she directed.

He held up one thigh, while pushing on the mother's belly. He could feel the baby's head moving downward.

"Keep pushing," Nora whispered.

The mother-in-law watched, her eyes round, her arms holding onto the mother's opposite thigh.

"Don't stop until the baby is completely out," Nora said, working her fingers around the baby's chin and the back of its head.

The mother whimpered, too tired and weak to cry out.

When Rucker thought it had been too long and the baby would surely die, the head popped through. He released the woman's leg and let go of the breath he'd been holding since he'd started pushing the baby's head.

Nora caught the baby. Holding it by the ankles, she turned it upside down in an attempt to clear its lungs. Still the baby didn't cry out, nor did it appear to be breathing.

Nora pressed the baby to her chest and rubbed his back vigorously, over and over.

Finally, the baby emitted a gurgling cough and let out a yell that made the mother sob.

Smiling, Nora laid the baby on the mother's chest. Then she delivered the afterbirth.

The mother-in-law took over, helping to clean up the mother and the bed. She handed a pair of scissors to Nora.

Nora glanced at Rucker. "You want to cut the umbilical cord?"

Rucker held up his hands. "Uh, no thank you. Besides, you were the one who did all the work."

"I'm just glad it turned out all right." Nora cut the umbilical cord and leaned over the mother and child. "Congratulations on your baby boy."

"*Daera manana,*" the woman said, smiling weakly at her baby. "Thank you."

"*Salaam aalaikum,*" Nora said, running her hand over the baby's head.

In English, Rucker repeated her sentiment. "Peace be with you."

Nora gave the woman instructions on caring for herself after giving birth and for the baby.

Rucker was in awe of all she'd done, and that she hadn't fallen apart in the middle of it. He would never admit it, but he was a bit shaken by the experience. They'd just delivered a breech baby in a war-torn country.

The door opened, and the father entered, his eyes wide and worried. "All is well?"

Nora nodded, peeling off her gloves. "Congratulations, you have a son, and your wife seems to be doing fine."

The frown creasing the man's forehead cleared. He hurried to his wife's side and peered down at the baby in her arms, a smile spreading across his face. "Allah is good." He looked up at Rucker and Nora. "*Daera manana*. Thank you."

Nora nodded.

"My apologies for taking you at gunpoint. I did not know how else to get you here." He held out his hand. "I am Pazir. My wife is Gulpari. We are in your debt for keeping my family alive."

"Why didn't you ask the base for help?" Nora asked.

Pazir shook his head. "The Taliban sees all. If I visit the base, they will assume I am passing secrets to the American forces. They will punish me by punishing my family."

Gulpari clutched her baby close. "We did not know what else to do."

Pazir sighed. "I took you at gunpoint as a show of force; the Taliban will not question."

"Are you a member of the Taliban?" Rucker asked.

The man looked away. "In their eyes, I am."

"In yours?" Rucker asked.

"To keep my family alive, I do what I have to."

Rucker's fists clenched. "Have you killed Americans?"

"No," Pazir said. "I believe Allah is kind and good. But I must walk among the Taliban."

Nora nodded. "I understand. I hope they don't read into our visit today anything other than the opportunity to help your wife in labor." She nodded toward Rucker. "Now, if you don't mind, we need to get back to the base before dark. My people will be worried and will send out squads of soldiers to look for us."

"Of course. I will take you back to the edge of the village, closest to the base."

Rucker nodded. "And provide cover while we drive away from town?"

Pazir nodded. "I owe you for saving my wife and son's lives. I will be forever in your debt." He gave a slight bow. "You will follow me to your vehicle. My men and I will ride with you until we get close."

"As long as they don't plan on shooting us in the back of our heads," Rucker said.

Pazir clasped his hands together and gave Rucker a slight bow. "You have my word. You and the nurse will be safe with us."

"And you'll give my driver his weapon back when

we get there," Nora said. It wasn't a question, but a demand.

"To show my sincerity, he can have it back now." Pazir pulled the handgun from a pocket buried in his loose clothing and handed it to Rucker.

Rucker ejected the magazine. It was still full. He shrugged into his uniform jacket, then his bulletproof vest and slid the handgun into the holster at his hip.

Nora slipped her jacket on over her bloodied T-shirt. "How did you know a nurse would be coming into town today?"

"We know," Pazir said. "If you are certain my wife will be all right, you can come with me now."

Nora looked toward the mother-in-law who had done a good job of cleaning up the mess of child-birth. The older woman gave her a sincere nod.

"She'll be all right as long as you keep her clean and germ-free. The same goes for the baby. Wash hands with soap and water that has had the bacteria boiled out of it before handling the baby."

Pazir spoke to his mother, and then nodded to Nora. "Follow me."

He led them out to where the HUMMV was parked in the walled yard. Nora checked the items in the back. When she was satisfied, she nodded.

"We only took the gloves." Pazir said something to the two men with the rifles.

One of them ran back into the house. A moment

later, he returned with the box of surgical gloves and handed them to Pazir.

He, in turn, handed the box to Nora. "Again, I thank you for saving my wife and son. I am indebted to you. I will find a way to repay that honor." He gave her a brief bow and waved a hand toward the HUMMV.

Rucker opened the door for her.

Nora climbed into the passenger seat.

After closing the door, Rucker hurried around to the driver's seat. He didn't completely trust the Afghans after they'd taken them at gunpoint.

The three men climbed into the back seat. This time their guns weren't pointed at Rucker and Nora's heads. The drive through the streets was a little less stressful, though Rucker knew the men could kill them if they wanted. The fact that Pazir considered himself part of the Taliban left Rucker uneasy. Even if he only belonged as an attempt to keep his family safe.

As he drove, Rucker studied the turns. Pazir took them a different route from the one that got them to his home in the first place. Rucker wasn't sure he could find his way back to the walled home.

Pazir was smart. He didn't want them retracing their route.

Soon, the Afghan had him stop. "We will leave you here. Follow the road ahead. It will take you to the main path leading back to the base. You will recognize it when you get there. Peace be with you."

The three men left the vehicle and disappeared down a crowded street.

Rucker shifted into drive and moved slowly forward, not liking that they were without an escort preceding and following them. Hopefully, they were close enough to the base they could make a run for it, if they found themselves attacked. He inched through the throngs of people until they arrived at the main, wider road he remembered driving down earlier that day. He turned toward the base. "I suppose the vaccinations will have to be done another day," he said.

Nora nodded. "It's getting late in the day and I have the night shift. I need to get a few hours of sleep before I go on duty. Besides, I want to give the children the time and attention they deserve."

Rucker nodded. "You really care about them, don't you?"

She gave him a sad smile. "I do. I hate leaving them. I wish I could take all of them home with me."

"You have a big heart. And what you did for that woman and her baby..." He shook his head. "Delivering a baby is hard enough, but delivering a breech baby..." He reached across and took her hand. "You were amazing."

She stared down at where his hand held hers without pulling away. "Thank you for helping."

"I only did what you told me. You were the star of that show." He winked.

She laughed softly. "I have to admit, I was shaking inside. That could have gone horribly wrong, ending in the death of the baby and the mother." She looked up at him. "That would've been bad. And if they'd died, I wasn't sure Pazir would let us live to come back to the base."

"You had a lot riding on the outcome." He squeezed her hand gently. "It all turned out for the best. And I think you made a friend out of a member of the Taliban."

Nora grimaced. "I'm not sure that's a good thing. What's to keep them from abducting me or one of the other nurses again?"

"Are you going to the orphanage tomorrow?" Rucker asked.

She nodded. "I have to. I don't have many days left here. I want to make sure those kids get the vaccinations they need."

He gave a single nod. "I'll arrange to be your driver again."

"Thanks for being there for me." She continued to hold his hand up until they drove up to the base gate. Then she pulled her fingers free and stared straight ahead.

After they showed their IDs and were let through, Rucker drove her directly to the medical facility. As soon as they arrived, it seemed like everyone inside flooded out into the open.

Captain Williams hurried forward with a couple Military Policemen. "Nora." She hugged Nora and stepped back. "Lieutenant Michaels. We had a search party out looking for you. What happened?"

"We were abducted by several Afghans." Nora looked to Rucker. "I'm tired and shaky. Could I get something to eat?"

"Absolutely." Captain Williams slipped an arm around her waist. "Did they hurt you in any way?"

"No." Nora gave a brief smile. "They wanted me to help deliver a baby."

"Dear, sweet Jesus," Captain Williams exclaimed.

A man in a white coat stepped forward. "Why didn't they just ask one of us to come help?"

"They had their reasons," Rucker said.

"You can tell them what happened. I really need to get something to eat."

Another nurse hurried forward. "Nora, come inside and sit down. I'll send one of the specialists to the chow hall for a tray."

"Thanks, Beth," Nora said.

The woman led her into the medical facility and urged her to take a seat.

Rucker followed and addressed the crowd gathering around. "Lieutenant Michaels helped a woman deliver a breech baby."

The medical staff all let out a collective gasp.

"Wow," Captain Williams said. "I've only helped deliver breech babies during a caesarean section."

"Same," the doctor in the white coat said. "And the baby's head didn't get stuck in the birth canal?"

Nora shook her head. "Sergeant Sloan applied pressure to the head as I eased the baby out. It was a textbook delivery, which was a good thing as that was the only knowledge I had of breech deliveries." She smiled. "It was a healthy baby boy."

The people gathered around clapped.

"Who were the men who took you? Did they give you names?" one of the MPs asked, a frown denting his forehead.

Nora's gaze met Rucker's as she answered. "No."

Rucker was glad she hadn't revealed the man's name. The last thing Pazir needed was for MPs to show up at his house and cause a ruckus. The Taliban could come down hard on him for whatever infraction they decided he'd incurred.

After they'd reported the incident to the MPs and Nora got something to eat, Rucker excused himself and hurried over to his commander to let him know he was back and unharmed.

He walked into his commander's office to find his team all gathered inside.

"Oh good, you're back." His commander said. "Thought we were going on a mission to rescue your ass. What was that all about, anyway?"

Rucker shook his head. His team had no idea he'd

been kidnapped and held at gunpoint to help deliver a baby. "It's not important. What's going on?"

"We've got orders from SOCOM," their commanding officer said. "They've located Abdul Akund. We've been tasked to surround his hideout and observe for twenty-four hours. We're to make sure our intelligence sources are correct, and he really is there before we make our move to capture him. They want minimal civilian casualties. Preferably none."

Rucker tensed. "When do we mobilize?"

"Tonight. We get in place and watch through the night and through tomorrow. If he's there, we make our move tomorrow night."

The mission meant he couldn't take Nora to the orphanage the next day. He had to let her know. He didn't like the idea of her going after what had happened that day, but he couldn't tell her what to do. He could ask her to wait a couple days until he was back from his mission.

Rucker shook his head. He could ask, but he already knew her answer.

She wouldn't wait.

She'd want to get those vaccines to the children, the sooner the better. The closer to her redeployment date she got, the more she'd want to tie up loose ends. He knew, as one who'd redeployed on multiple occasions, how important it felt to wrap up the projects he'd started.

"Grab your gear, eat chow, shit, shower, shave and whatever else you need to do to be ready for a mission that could take twenty-four to forty-eight hours. Meet back here in one hour for your briefing and orders." The commander clapped his hands together. "Dismissed."

The team left the building. Rucker fell in step between Dash and Bull.

"Wow, sounds like you had a helluva day," Dash said.

"Why the hell are you at this briefing?" Rucker demanded. "Shouldn't you be recuperating for another forty-eight hours?"

"I'm fine," his friend said. "Besides, I want that bastard. After what he put me through, I want a piece of him."

"I don't think it's a good idea to take on so much after having a head injury," Rucker argued. "You should sit this one out and let us find the guy and bring him back for you."

"We tried to reason with him. The hit to his head must have been harder than we thought," Bull said, shaking his head.

"Or he's just that hardheaded," Dawg said behind them.

"He's hardheaded all right," Tank said.

"You'd feel the same," Dash argued. "Won't be nearly as satisfying unless I'm there when he's captured."

Rucker shrugged.

"You didn't answer me," Dash said. "What happened to you today? Did you drive the pretty lieutenant out to the orphanage."

"I tried. We were cut off from our escorts, then taken at gunpoint to a home in town where Nora was forced to deliver a breech baby, and I helped. Just another day at the office." Rucker walked with Dash toward the chow hall.

"Holy shit, Ruck. Why didn't you tell the commander what happened?" Dash asked.

"What the ever-loving-hell?" Bull exclaimed. "You helped deliver a baby?"

Tank chuckled. "Unbelievable."

Lance asked, "Everything come out all right?"

Rucker nodded. "Nora was amazing. She knew exactly what to do and had me help deliver the baby."

"Wow," Dawg said. "Did they say why they took you at gunpoint? I assume they let you go after the baby was delivered or you wouldn't be here now."

"They did." Rucker's brow pinched. "I'm surprised the MPs didn't let the commander know I'd been taken." Rucker entered the chow hall, realizing he was hungry after spending the entire day delivering a baby. At least he got to spend it with Nora. And she'd been amazing getting that baby out alive.

"None of us knew you were in trouble," Lance said.

"That's right," Bull nodded. "You got back about the time you said you would."

Tank grabbed a tray and started loading it with food. "If you hadn't shown up for the briefing, we would've asked about you and why you were late."

Rucker took the next tray and followed Tank down the line. "By then, I could've been in the next province."

"Yet, here you are," Dash said, joining them with his tray loaded with food.

When the team took seats at a table and dug into their food, Rucker filled them in on exactly what had happened.

Bull whistled when he finished. "The important things to remember from that little exercise is Pazir now owes you a debt of honor, and there are spies on this base reporting to a member of the Taliban."

"Don't forget," Dawg said, "Rucker now knows how to deliver babies."

"No." Rucker shook his head. "Lieutenant Michaels knows how to deliver babies. I was just doing what she told me to do."

"We'll keep all those factoids in our back pockets for a rainy day," Dash said. "You never know when you'll need a friend in the Taliban."

"And we can't be too open about what we say or do on this base," Blade noted.

"Or when you need to pinch hit a breech birth." Mac chuckled.

"Don't laugh," Rucker said. "I never even thought I'd need such a skill."

Dash grinned. "Well, now you're the team expert on birthing babies."

"Eat up," Rucker said. "We have to get moving in order to get ready for this little shindig." He had to get to Nora and let her know he couldn't go with her the next day to the orphanage. What were the chances she'd wait until he could go with her?

CHAPTER 6

Nora had just made it back to her quarters after being fed at the medical facility. Her medical team had congratulated her and asked a lot of questions about her experience being kidnapped at gunpoint, and then delivering a breech baby without any medical support or a doctor to perform a caesarean section.

All she wanted to do now was get back to her bed, relax and try to sleep before she had to report to duty for the graveyard shift.

Beth was in their quarters when she got there.

"Thanks for leaving me at the mercy of that mob," Nora said.

Beth gave her a crooked smile as she dragged a brush through her damp hair. "Sorry. I didn't think I could get them to stop long enough to get you out, so

I came back here. My shift was over, and I needed a shower."

Nora glanced down at her soiled clothing. "I could use one myself."

"Go. I'll light some candles and make it Zen in here so you can relax and get ready to sleep."

"Thanks."

"Then you can tell me the important stuff, like how it was with Mr. Macho driving you into danger."

Nora's chest contracted. Even though they'd been held at gunpoint, she'd felt safer just having Rucker there with her the whole time.

"I can see by your expression that you liked having him around." Her friend waved at her. "Go. Get that shower so you can come back and spill about the boy."

Nora stripped out of her stained uniform, tossed on her terrycloth bathrobe, gathered her things for the trip to the shower and hurried out the door.

Ten minutes later, she was back, hair dripping and feeling a little better now that she had scrubbed away the last of the dust and blood from her adventure.

Nora sat at her makeshift desk with the mirror hung over it and pulled her brush through the tangles in her hair.

"Here. Let me." Beth took her brush from her and worked the tangles free. "So, did he really help, or did he pass out at the sight of blood?"

Nora sighed. "He was amazing. He was right there assisting without making faces or throwing up."

"Score one for the cute guy."

"I couldn't have delivered that baby without his help."

"I'll have to remember that next time I need an assistant to help me deliver a baby," Beth said with a smile. "Too bad you're leaving so soon. Think I might have a shot at him once you're gone?"

Nora twisted in her seat, frowning. "Seriously?"

"Well, you *are* leaving. And he might get lonely..." Beth laughed and went back to brushing Nora's hair. "Don't worry. I won't try to steal your guy. It's clear that he only has eyes for you."

Nora stared at her friend in the mirror. "You really think so?"

"Sweetie, the man arranged to be your driver for the day. If that doesn't say love, I don't know what does."

Nora sighed. "It doesn't matter. I'm leaving soon. He's enlisted, and it's not like we can have a fling before I go. I don't want to ruin my career over a cute guy."

"If you're going to ruin your career, it might as well be over a cute guy versus one who's not so cute." Beth chuckled. "I think we've been here too long. It's time to get back to the States where you can date and get laid without worrying you'll get court-martialed."

"No kidding."

"Too bad Sergeant Sloan isn't going back at the same time."

"Hell, I don't even know where he shipped out from," Nora said.

"Have you told him where you're going?" Beth smoothed Nora's hair and started dividing the wet strands to weave into a French braid.

"He said he was going to take me to the orphanage tomorrow since we didn't make it there today."

"Cool. You could find somewhere to get a little nooky in along the way."

"Beth!"

Beth held up her hands. "I know. You're not that kind of girl. But sometimes, don't you wish you were?"

Nora stared at herself in the mirror.

Yes. She wished she was. Being a rule follower was a burden she wished she didn't feel obligated to bear.

"It would be nice to at least know how he kisses," Beth mused. "The whole affair could end before it started if he was a lousy kisser."

Nora's lips tingled. Based on the one kiss he'd stolen, she knew he was a good kisser.

Beth's eyes widened. "You've kissed him."

Nora frowned. "Technically, no."

"Technically?" Beth laughed. "There's no technically about it. You have that look of a woman who's been kissed."

Nora touched her cheek. "I didn't kiss him. He kissed me."

"And by the simple fact you didn't bring him up on sexual harassment charges, I'd say you liked it." Beth's grin broadened. "When did he do it? After you two delivered the baby?" Her smile twisted. "Though how you could exchange a kiss when men with guns stood over you, I don't know."

"No. There wasn't time to kiss today. He kissed me when I went in early for my shift and checked on his friend." Her pulse pounded at the memory. "I didn't expect it. It just happened."

"Man, you're in trouble."

Nora bit her bottom lip. "I know. I could lose my commission for not saying something about it."

"Or you could lose your commission by saying something. And if you liked it, you're better off not saying anything."

"I'm torn." Nora turned to her friend. "If there weren't so many rules, it would be different."

"But there are, and that's what's bothering you." Beth sat on the edge of her cot. "You are in between a rock and a hard place. And you're leaving in a few days." Her brow twisted. "I'm going to miss you."

Nora reached for her friend's hand. "I'm going to miss you, too. But we'll keep in touch."

"And the military is a small world. We'll see each other again. You can bank on that."

"I hope so."

A knock sounded on her door.

Beth hopped up. "I'll get it. It's probably the MPs wanting to ask more questions."

Nora turned back to the mirror, took up her brush and then laid it back down. Beth had done a great job French braiding her hair, and she didn't wear makeup to work.

"Sergeant Sloan, what brings you to our little hovel?" Beth said loudly.

Nora's heart leaped into her throat, and her fingers clenched the edge of the little desk.

"I need to talk to Nor—Lieutenant Michaels. Is she here?"

"Why yes, she is." Beth glanced over at Nora. "I was just on my way over to the chow hall for a cup of tea. I'm sure she'd love to see you." Beth left the door open as she exited their quarters.

Nora leaped to her feet, wishing she'd put on something more than the T-shirt and shorts she'd worn from the shower unit.

At least her hair was brushed and braided.

Rucker moved into the doorway but didn't come all the way inside. "How are you?"

She dipped her head. "Okay. How are you?"

He didn't smile. "Okay."

For a long moment, neither said anything. Nora stared at him, wanting to fill her memory with his handsome face. Before long, she'd be on her way back to the States, and he'd still be here. The thought made her very sad, when she was supposed to be glad to be on her way home.

Home.

She really didn't have a home. Not since her mother died. Home was wherever she hung her hat. At that moment, it happened to be in Afghanistan.

With Rucker.

Only he wasn't hers to be with. And Afghanistan wasn't the place they could be together.

"I'm glad you came by—" she started.

"I came because I needed—" he said at the same time. He smiled. "You go first."

"No, you go first." She had been about to tell him that he couldn't drive her to the orphanage. If they were seen together too often, when he really had no reason to be with her, it could get them both in trouble.

"I'm sorry, Nora, but I can't take you to the orphanage tomorrow," he said. "Is there any way you can put it off for two days? I can do it then. We're being tasked with a mission."

Her heart squeezed hard in her chest. Even though she'd been about to tell him he couldn't take her to the orphanage, she was sad and disappointed that he'd backed out first. "Don't worry about it. It's probably best that you don't take me anyway."

"The thing is, I'm worried. After what happened

today, I'm afraid it'll happen again. You were cut off from your escorts, and I wasn't enough to keep you safe."

"It all worked out fine in the end," Nora said. "And the more we're seen together, the more people will talk. I don't want to get you in trouble."

"And I don't want you to get into trouble because you're seeing me." He moved fully into the building. "But I want to see you. I can't stop thinking about you. You've been in my thoughts and on my mind since we played volleyball."

"And had coffee together," she finished softly. "I shouldn't say this, but it's been the same for me." She shook her head. "But it can't be. Not here."

"What about when we get back to the States?" he asked. "Can I look you up?"

The thought of seeing him back in the States made her heart flutter with excitement. They would still have the same issues. He was enlisted. She was an officer. It wasn't unheard of for a couple to fall in love like that, but it was highly frowned upon, mostly if they were in the same chain of command.

She started to shake her head.

He held up his hand. "Don't answer that yet. Wait until we're both back in the U.S. In the meantime, if you don't go to the orphanage tomorrow, and I'm back before you go, I'd be honored if you'd allow me to be your driver." He touched his hand to his chest.

"I'm going tomorrow, unless it rains." Her lips

twitched into a smile. "And the chances of rain are slim to none."

He nodded. "I understand."

Did he? He probably thought she didn't want to be with him, when the opposite was true. She wanted it more than she could tell him. But it wasn't right. Not by military standards. Not here.

He held out his hand. "If I don't see you before you leave, I'd like to leave you with a handshake."

She stared at his hand, almost afraid to take it. But what could a handshake do to her? Nothing.

She laid her hand in his and immediately knew the error of the gesture.

That simple touch shot electric current throughout her body, leaving her shaking inside with the force of her desire to take him in her arms and kiss him deeply. She gulped hard to dislodge the lump in her throat and whispered, "Goodbye."

He shook his head. "Not goodbye..." Rucker stared into her eyes. "Until we see each other again." Then he lifted her hand to his mouth and pressed his lips to the backs of her knuckles.

She froze, her heart stopping for a second, her breath catching in her throat.

Then he turned her hand over and pressed another kiss into her palm. "Save that one for later, to remember me by." He curled her fingers around her palm, released her hand and left.

He left, but he took an integral part of her with him.

CHAPTER 7

"I COULD USE A BEER ABOUT NOW," Dash said into Rucker's ear.

"Me, too," Rucker echoed. They'd been in position outside the village their intel had identified as Akund's latest hideout. They'd staked out the little town shortly before sunrise and had been in place for the past five hours. No one had entered or left the village in that time. Not one vehicle, donkey or person on foot.

Rucker was positioned on a rocky knoll close to the road with Dash, Mac, Blade, Lance and Tank spread out further in a semicircle curving toward the village.

Dawg held a sniper position on higher ground, overlooking the road and the entry into the village. Bull was even higher up, observing the village from a bird's eye view.

As men of action, they had to be just as frustrated with waiting and observing as Rucker.

"The little bar outside the main gate at Ft. Hood has the best selection of beer," Dawg offered. "I like when we get them ice cold after a hot day in the field."

"I want a hamburger," Tank said. "With all the fixin's."

"And an order of fries covered with chili and cheese," Tank said.

"You'd ruin good fries with cheese?" Blade's voice came over the radio headset.

"Lance, isn't your enlistment up in a couple of months?" Dash asked.

"Yeah," Lance answered. "So?"

"Are you going to re-up?" Dash asked.

Rucker wanted to know the answer to that question as well. His enlistment would come to an end in five more months. Until now, he hadn't considered getting out. He was proud to be a part of Delta Force. The team was his family. The job was important, and he was good at what he did.

But being on the team meant sacrificing a personal life. Those who dared to have a family and be a member of Delta Force sacrificed family time when they were called up to perform a mission.

They missed out on a lot of the milestones of their kids' lives, from their first steps to their high school graduations. Not to mention the missed birthdays for the kids and their wives. Many ended up divorced, rarely seeing their kids. Why any of the members of the Delta Force would get married was a mystery to Rucker.

Until now.

Until Nora.

Not that Rucker knew her well enough to think they should get married and raise a litter of kids, but if they could spend more time together, it might lead to something.

Nora would make beautiful children. Not only would they be beautiful, they'd be loved. Nora loved children, and she cared enough to look out for their happiness. Plus, she understood the military. If you were called to deploy, you went.

Too many of the guys married women who'd never been around military men. Hell, many of them had never been outside their home state, much less halfway across the country. They didn't understand the level of commitment it took to be with a man who could be gone three months to a year at a time.

"Hadn't really thought about it," Lance said. "But now that you mention it, maybe it's time to look into buying that ranch I said I always wanted. Even if I don't get out, it wouldn't hurt to find my retirement home and get it paid off before I leave the military."

"A ranch?" Dash laughed. "Since when are you a rancher?"

"I've done my share of ranching," Lance said. "I

spent summers working for my uncle who owns six hundred acres in east Texas. He has a hundred head of cattle, horses, goats and pigs. I know a little about what it takes to keep them fed and healthy."

"What about you, Rucker?" Dawg said. "Aren't you coming up on your re-enlistment before the end of the year?"

"Yeah," Rucker said.

"And?" Dawg persisted.

"I'm still thinking about it," Rucker said.

"You're not seriously considering leaving the team, are you?" Dash asked.

"I hadn't," Rucker said.

"Until now?" Dash knew him too well.

"Thinking about the pretty lieutenant who's teaching you how to deliver babies?" Blade asked.

"No. But I am thinking about my future. There will come a day when we're too old to perform this kind of work."

"Dude, that's when you retire," Bull said. "You're not that old or decrepit."

"No, but if I wait until I retire to do the other things I want, it'll be too late."

"Like what?" Blade asked.

"Like find a woman, get married and have a handful of kids."

"Marriage is overrated," Tank said. "Over half end in divorce."

"Hey, you poking at me?" Blade demanded.

"No," Tank said. "Just stating facts."

"Good thing. I'd hate to have to rearrange your face," Blade said.

"You and whose army?" Tank retorted.

"This is all about the lieutenant, isn't it?" Dash asked.

"No," Rucker lied. "It could be about any female I might want to settle down with. Why bother if I'm never around to maintain a decent relationship?"

"Exactly," Blade interjected. "My marriage didn't even last through the first deployment."

"Your wife wasn't cut out to be married to a man in uniform," Bull said. "She'd never been away from her family. Hell, her mother came to live with you the first year you two were married. That relationship was doomed from the start. How did you two meet in the first place?"

"She was my high school sweetheart," Blade said. "She told me she wanted to see the world."

Tank snorted. "The world isn't Ft. Hood, Texas."

"The part she didn't tell you was that she wanted to see the world in short trips and return to her hometown every time," Rucker said. "She wasn't used to being away from the only home she'd ever known."

"True," Blade said. "I'm just glad we never had kids."

"So, Ruck, what would you do if you quit the team?" Bull asked.

"I'd finish my business degree, start up a security agency and hire all of you slugs to provide security for my clients."

"Sign me up for when I retire," Blade said. "I'll need something to keep me busy, and I figure I'll have another twenty to thirty good years left in me even after I get out."

"Same with me," Tank said. "Will we get to carry guns?"

Rucker shrugged. "I'd think so."

"Think that will win over your nurse?" Blade asked.

Would his nurse still be single? Hell. Would she be interested? Rucker wasn't even sure she was interested now. Although she hadn't pushed him away when he'd kissed her, she hadn't responded. But then again, he'd surprised her.

"Vehicles approaching the village," Dash said.

The chatter ceased.

A single truck approached.

Rucker brought a pair of binoculars up to his eyes and studied the occupants. "One driver, no passengers. The truck appears to be carrying small boxes. Possibly containing supplies for a store."

"Or ammunition and explosives," Bull offered.

More vehicles came and went from the village, each appearing to be driven by civilians coming and going. No truckloads of militants or dark SUVs carrying Taliban leaders.

The day went by so slowly, Rucker ground several layers of enamel off his teeth wondering what was happening with Nora.

Had she made it to the orphanage safely?

In the afternoon, three trucks approached the village. Two led the procession in front of a dark SUV. One followed. The heavily tinted windows of the SUV made it difficult for Rucker to see inside to know who had just arrived. "No one in that village can afford an SUV like that," he said into his mic. "Bull, what have you got?"

Bull had a better position from another hilltop to see down into the village. "They just pulled to a stop in front of the largest house. There are men in black turbans climbing out of the driver's seat and the front passenger seat."

Rucker strained to see what he couldn't. The walls of the village blocked his view from his vantage point.

"Two men just got out of the back. One on each side. They're waiting... Another man is getting out." Bull paused for so long Rucker thought he might have gone to sleep.

"It looks like our guy, Abdul Akund."

Rucker let go of the breath he'd held for the length of Bull's report. They could get in, take him and get out in under an hour, if all went well.

"He's going into the building," Bull said. "We could have some issues."

"What issues?"

"There appears to be a celebration taking place nearby. A wedding, maybe. Seems every civilian in town is attending."

"Great," Dash said. "Civilians."

Rucker's hands tightened into fists. "We wait until the wedding crowd disperses." Night was best for fewer civilian casualties anyway. Afghans went to sleep when the sun went down. Few people wandered around to get in the way,

"As long as our guy doesn't bug out before then," Bull said.

"Keep your eyes peeled," Rucker said. "If he moves, we close in on his exit route and take him out there."

They waited, Bull watching and keeping them informed of the progress of the wedding party and the building into which Akund had disappeared.

As the sun sank below the horizon, Rucker prepared for action.

"Looks like the crowd is dispersing," Bull reported. "The bride and groom went into a building."

"We need to be ready to move as soon as the streets clear," Rucker said.

"Wait," Bull said, his voice tense. "Some men came out of the house and got into the SUV. I counted five. I couldn't tell if one of them was our man. There isn't enough light down there to tell. There are others climbing into two of the trucks that accompanied the SUV into the village."

"He arrived in that vehicle," Dash said. "He's probably leaving in it."

"Agreed. We'll converge on the road and set up our welcoming committee," Rucker said. "Bull, stay put unless we need assistance. Let us know if the village people mobilize to help Akund's caravan."

"Roger. Will comply."

"Dawg, you got our six?"

"Got a clear view of the road and our guys," Dawg said. "Gotcha covered."

"Bring it in. Let's do this." Rucker moved into position closer to the road with a detonator in hand. Early that morning, before sunup, they'd rigged the road in several places with explosives enough to disable vehicles passing over without necessarily killing those inside.

Rucker waited for the lead vehicles loaded with armed men to roll past the first set of explosives. Once the SUV reached them, he hit the detonator. Explosions rocked the ground around them.

The trucks full of armed men jerked to a halt, the tires destroyed. The men in the cabs and those in the back leaped to the ground and started firing into the dusk.

The team took them out with minimal effort and closed in on the damaged SUV.

Up until that point, no one had exited the vehicle.

Rucker called out, using what little Pashto he'd learned, telling the occupants of the vehicles to get out.

When nothing happened, Rucker aimed his weapon at the SUV's front engine compartment and let loose several rounds, piercing the metal.

The front doors of the SUV burst open. Two men bailed out, hit the ground and rolled over, firing rifles.

Thankfully, there was still enough residual light in the sky that Rucker and his team could see the men to take them out.

Then the back door of the SUV flew open and an older man stepped out, raising his hand into the air.

"Do not shoot!" he cried in heavily accented English. "Do not shoot!"

"Everyone out of the vehicle," Rucker shouted.

The man with his hands in the air said something to the people inside the vehicle.

Slowly, the occupants climbed out. One other man and a woman, dressed in what appeared to be the traditional Afghan wedding garment, an ornate green dress, signifying purity.

Rucker addressed the older man. "Abdul Akund, where is he?"

"We do not know. He insisted we take his vehicle and escort. He took ours."

Rucker cursed. "Bull. Was there another vehicle leaving the village in a different direction?"

"There is now. Leaving to the west out of a small side street, taking a dirt path along the base of the hills."

"The road leads into the hills," the older man said. "Once in the hills, he will be difficult to find."

"Dash, get our transport here ASAP."

They had been dropped via Black Hawk helicopters a couple miles away from the village and had walked the rest of the way early that morning.

The Black Hawks had returned to base but were on standby. Unfortunately, they wouldn't be there soon enough to catch up to Akund. Akund's SUV and the escort vehicle that accompanied the bride and groom were disabled and of no use to them to catch up to Akund in the hills.

Rucker cursed. Once again, the Taliban leader had outsmarted them.

"Why was Akund here?" Rucker demanded.

The old man blinked. "For the wedding. He is the uncle of the bride. He came to give the bride his blessing for the wedding."

The Deltas released the bride, groom and the groom's father to return to the village and seek alternate transportation to their new home in another village.

Within twenty minutes, the Army Black Hawks arrived. The Delta Force team loaded into them and took off.

On the ride back, Rucker played the mission back

in his mind like an instant replay of a football game. As he did, his fists clenched.

He hated when a mission failed by their own actions or because the intelligence information was incomplete. What he hated worse was when the enemy knew they were coming and set a trap that hurt his teammates. Whatever it took, Akund had to die.

CHAPTER 8

THE CHOPPER LANDED at the base just short of midnight.

As soon as the men disembarked and the CO debriefed them in the operations room, Rucker hurried to the medical facility.

Every minute of the longest day of his life, his thoughts had been with Nora, wondering if she'd made it to the orphanage and back all right.

As he neared the medical facility, a crowd was gathered around comprised of the medical staff, several dozen soldiers armed to the teeth and the base commander.

Rucker's gut knotted. He found Nora's roommate and Captain Williams, the head nurse, standing close together, holding hands.

He headed straight for them.

When they saw him, both women had the same

expressions. Their eyes rounded, and they rushed toward him, both talking at once.

"Sergeant Sloan, thank God you're back," the captain said.

"Rucker, Nora..." Beth said and swallowed a sob. "She's gone."

"What?" Rucker stared from one woman to the other.

The captain's face looked ten years older, with lines etched deeply into her forehead and her eyes red-rimmed as if she'd been crying. She drew in a deep, shaky breath. "They took her."

Rucker gripped the woman's shoulders. "Who took Nora?"

"Men dressed in black outfits and turbans. They had guns. They took Nora and the orphans. We didn't know it was happening. We were too late to stop them." The captain brushed tears from her cheeks.

Beth grabbed Rucker's arm. "You have to get her back. There's no telling what they'll do to her."

"I don't know what you can do, but if you can do anything, please...do it soon," Captain Williams said.

"Start by telling me just what happened," Rucker said, drawing deep breaths to calm his racing heart.

The captain took a steadying breath. "We were wrapping things up at the orphanage. We were all in the vehicles to go back to the base when Nora remembered she'd left her stethoscope in the room we'd been using inside." Her voice caught on a sob. "When she didn't come right back, the soldiers went looking for her." She shook her head.

"What happened?" Rucker said, wanting to shake the words out of the nurse's mouth.

"They searched the orphanage. It was empty. No one was there. When they went out the back door, they spotted a truck. A man was loading someone into the back. That someone was wearing a desert camouflage uniform. Sweet Jesus, it was Lieutenant Michaels." Captain Williams sucked in a breath and continued. "The soldiers couldn't shoot for fear of hitting the lieutenant. We tried to follow them, but they drove into the village and lost us in all the twists and turns."

"She's gone," Beth said. "And she was supposed to go home in a couple of days. I knew she shouldn't have gone to that orphanage."

"We went back to the orphanage. The staff had reappeared and were talking to the Afghan police force. We discovered that the men in the truck had taken the orphans. All of them."

"And Nora," Beth looked up at Rucker. "Why would they have taken a bunch of little girls?"

Rucker's lips thinned into a tight line. "Girls sell for a lot more than boys in sex trafficking rings."

Captain Williams clamped a hand over her mouth. "Those poor babies. Poor Nora."

"We'll get them back," Rucker promised. "Right

now, I need to talk to my people." He left the crowd at the medical facility and ran back to his CO's operations room. He was still there, only he was talking to the base commander.

Rucker came to a halt and stood at attention. "Sir, permission to speak?"

Both commanders turned toward him.

"Go ahead," his CO said.

"One of the nurses was taken from a local orphanage today. I volunteer for the mission to retrieve her."

"Good," his CO said. "I was just working out with the base commander how we were going to find where they've taken her. We'll need to get with the intelligence guys and have them study the satellite images and work with their men on the ground to see if there's any news on their whereabouts."

"I might have another source of intel," Rucker said.

"Who?" the base commander asked.

"I can't say, but if you'll give me permission to leave the base, I'll find him and see if he knows where they went."

"You have my permission," the base commander said. "In the meantime, I'll work with the local leaders and see if they have any information. I doubt they will, but I have to show I'm taking it through the leadership chain." The base commander left the room.

Rucker waited impatiently for the man to close the door behind him. "Sir, I want to take Dash, if he's up to it, and Bull with me to talk with a local by the name of Pazir. If anyone in this area knows anything about the kidnapping, he would be the man."

His CO nodded. "Keep it on the downlow. If you're not back in a couple of hours, we're sending the rest of the team after you. Get a tracking device on each of you. I can't afford to lose one, much less three of my guys."

"Yes, sir." Rucker spun and reached for the door handle.

"And, Sloan..."

He turned back to his commander. "Sir?"

"I hope we find the nurse," he said. "I understand she's special to you."

"Yes, sir. She's smart, brave and a badass on the volleyball court."

"And she's an officer."

Rucker gave his CO a quick nod. "I know the ramifications of fraternization, sir."

"It won't only affect your career, it could ruin hers. If you really care for her, you'll keep everything aboveboard."

"Roger," Rucker said. He left the building and ran for the quarters he and his team had been assigned for their short stay. He found Dash stripping out of his uniform in their shared unit. "Your day isn't done. I need you and Bull to come with me. We'll need to be dressed like shadows and camouflaged for a night intelligence gathering mission."

"When?" Dash asked, pulling a long-sleeved black T-shirt out of his duffel bag.

"As soon as I can grab Bull and get camoed up." He left his unit and ran three doors down to the one Bull and Lance had been assigned.

He banged on the door.

Lance yanked it open. "Where's the fire?"

"I need Bull."

Bull looked over Lance's shoulder. He'd stripped down to his shorts. "What's up?"

"We have an assignment. Meet me in my unit dressed for night ops, black."

"Gonna tell me what it's all about?"

"Yeah, and why just the three of you?" Lance asked.

"Small detail. I don't have time to explain," Rucker said. "Don't worry. We'll need the entire team soon. Get a few minutes rest and be ready when we get back."

"I'll let the others know to hang close for potential mobilization," Lance said.

Rucker ran back to his quarters and burst through the door.

Dash was already dressed for the occasion and had his weapons laid out along with Rucker's. He was in the process of rubbing a stick of black camouflage over his face.

Rucker removed his armored vest and ripped off the desert camouflage jacket he'd needed to blend in with the dry terrain of Afghanistan during the day. He pulled on black, heavy-weight pants with cargo pockets on the legs. Pulling a black turtleneck shirt over his head, he tucked it into his trousers, shrugged into his armored vest and caught the camo stick Dash had been using. He slashed black camouflage paint over his face and hands.

Bull entered their unit without knocking, dressed in similar clothing and carrying his weapons.

After a brief breakdown of what had happened that day to Lieutenant Michaels and the girls from the orphanage, Rucker told the two what they were about to do.

"We're going into the village to speak to a member of the Taliban to ask where they would have taken the nurse and the girls from the orphanage."

Dash and Bull didn't question his sanity, only nodded.

As they left Rucker's quarters, they ran into their CO.

"You'll need these." He handed a set of keys to Rucker.

"What do they go to?" Rucker asked.

"A van the locals use to bring in supplies to the base. You don't want to drive a US military vehicle down those streets at night. You'd be a target before you went outside the wire. You'll find it parked by the PX. They like to keep it on the base so people won't steal it or stuff off it, like product, tires and batteries."

"Thank you, sir," Rucker said.

"And each of you put one of these in your shoe, your pocket...somewhere you won't lose it." He handed each one of the men a small round GPS tracking device.

"Two hours," the CO said, "and we're coming for you."

"Two hours will be sufficient," Rucker reassured him, praying he could find his way back to Pazir's home in the narrow streets at night.

Rucker, Dash and Bull followed the CO's instructions and found a decrepit van parked beside the mini post exchange where they could purchase shaving cream, razors and other necessities, along with the occasional candy bar or novel.

"I'll drive," Bull said.

Rucker handed him the keys, thankful the big guy offered. He rustled around the back of the van and found several small white tablecloths. He handed one to each of the men. "Wear it on your head. It might help to disguise us as we drive through the streets."

He slipped into the front passenger seat, and Dash knelt on the floor between them, his handgun at the ready.

Rucker held his Glock in his lap where he could reach it quickly.

The roads and turns were harder to find in the dark, though easier since there were no people to block their way.

After several missed turns, they finally pulled onto the street where Pazir's walled residence was located.

"Park there." Rucker pointed to a narrow alley between the crude mud and stick buildings.

Bull backed the van into the narrow space as far as he could, hiding it in the shadows.

The men tossed aside the tablecloths, climbed out of the van and followed the alley to the road that led behind Pazir's home.

No one moved in the darkness except the three Deltas. They clung to the shadows, slipping silently toward the walled home.

Rucker reached the wall first then stopped and listened.

On the other side, he heard people moving about, talking in hushed tones.

Dash cupped his hands, and Rucker stepped into them then pulled himself up onto the wall. He lay flat against the top, scanning the area. He couldn't see the front of the home from his position, but there were dim lights shining through the windows.

A baby cried inside. A woman's voice soothed it.

Bull climbed up on the wall behind Rucker. Together, they reached down and pulled Dash up between them.

Rucker dropped to the ground between the wall and the home. He eased up to one of the chest-high windows, pushed the glass inward and peered inside. The room he looked into was a sitting room he remembered passing by when he'd been led in and out of the house at gunpoint. A rug lay rolled against the wall, and pillows had been stacked by the door. Pictures and tapestries that had hung the day before were stacked neatly beside the rug.

Ducking low, he moved past the window toward the front of the house, pausing at the corner.

A truck stood in the yard, with furniture and household items stacked in the back and on the ground beside it.

Two men moved things out of the house into the truck.

One of them was Pazir. He hurried, barking orders in a quiet yet urgent tone. When he went back into the house, Rucker returned to the window looking into the sitting room.

Again, Dash cupped his hands, giving Rucker a boost up to the edge of the small window. Using Dash and Bull for leverage, Rucker squeezed through, dropped onto his hands on the other side and rolled to his feet.

Fortunately, no one came running or seemed to notice the little bit of noise he'd created getting through the window.

He hurried toward the door, stood to one side and waited to catch Pazir alone.

When that moment came, he slipped out behind the man, clamped an arm around the man's arms and his hand on his mouth. Then he pulled Pazir into the empty sitting room.

Pazir struggled, fighting to be free.

It was all Rucker could do to hold onto him. "It's me, the man who helped deliver your baby yesterday. If you promise not to yell, I'll let go of you. Promise?"

The man stopped moving and nodded.

As soon as Rucker released him, he sprang away, spun and faced Rucker.

Rucker held up a hand. "I'm not here to hurt anyone. I need to know about what happened at the orphanage today. Where did they take the nurse?"

Pazir shook his head. "I do not know."

"They took Lieutenant Michaels," Rucker said. "We want her back. Alive."

Pazir raked a hand through his hair. "I must get my family somewhere safe. If I hear of where they have taken her, I will send word. I cannot promise you when."

Rucker grabbed Pazir's arms. "The longer we wait, the less chance we have of finding her. I need to know where they are taking her tonight." He let go of the man as a female voice called out, "Pazir."

A young woman carrying a baby stepped into the sitting room.

Rucker recognized her as Pazir's wife, who'd given birth to the baby the day before. She walked slowly and held the baby clutched to her chest. When she spotted Rucker dressed all in black, his face painted black and scary, she opened her mouth to scream.

Pazir reached out and covered her mouth with his hand, speaking in a low, urgent tone.

She nodded. When he moved his hand away from her mouth, she spoked softly. "You are the one who help us?"

Rucker nodded.

Her husband spoke to her again.

She frowned and said something back.

Pazir spoke in Pashto again, his tone harsher.

Gulpari held her baby out for her husband to see and nodded toward Rucker.

Pazir sighed and turned to face him. "I will send my family ahead of me and stay to find out where they are taking the children and the nurse. Then I will have fulfilled my debt to you and the lieutenant."

"How will you get word to me?" Rucker asked.

"I will send word to you on your base."

Rucker didn't ask how he would do that. Based on the fact they knew what was going on and what US forces were moving and where they were headed, Pazir had his sources. He had to have faith that Pazir's word was good.

A man called out in the hallway.

Pazir jerked his head to the side, indicating Rucker should hide behind the door.

Pazir stepped out into the hallway and addressed the man helping him load his family's possessions. The man responded and kept walking down the hallway.

Pazir reentered the room and looked from Rucker to the window and back. "You came through the window?"

Rucker nodded.

"Come, you can exit through the back door." Pazir looked both ways in the hall before motioning Rucker to follow him.

His wife stayed back and waylaid the other man when he came back in from outside in the front yard.

At the end of the hallway was a kitchen with a door leading out the back way into a small garden with wilted vines.

Rucker turned to Pazir. "The sooner we know where to find her," he reiterated, "the sooner we can bring her back."

Pazir nodded. "I will do what I can. You will hear from me before morning." He turned and went back into his home, leaving Rucker to find his own way out of the walled residence.

Dash and Bull emerged from the shadows.

"So, we wait?" Bull asked.

Rucker's hands curled into fists. "Yes. We have no other leads on where she could have gone. If intel doesn't come up with something, we're completely dependent on Pazir to provide the information we need."

"Nothing like depending on the Taliban to give you useful information," Bull remarked.

"What are the chances Pazir will come through?" Dash asked.

Rucker cupped his hands as he stood beside the wall. "Good. We did him a huge favor. He owes me, and he owes Lieutenant Michaels even more. She saved his wife and son's lives."

Dash stepped into Rucker's hands and pulled himself up onto the wall. After he looked around, he whispered, "Clear."

Rucker held his hands together for Bull to climb up on the wall. Once there, he and Dash reached down and pulled Rucker up to straddle the wall between them. They dropped to the ground on the other side.

Moving through the shadows, they found the van where they'd left it, untouched. Slipping the white tablecloths over their heads, they drove through the streets and back to the base to wait for word from Pazir.

Once inside the base's concertina wire, Rucker headed for the CO's operations center. His commander was there on the phone with someone. When Rucker, Dash and Bull entered, he ended his call and shook his head. "Intel has nothing. What did you learn from your source?"

"Nothing," Rucker said. "Yet. He'll send word when he finds out where they took the Lieutenant and the children."

"You trust this source?"

"Sir, I do." He had to. Pazir was their only hope.

CHAPTER 9

NORA GATHERED the little girls close to her as they cried and shook. They were so scared and had every right to be. Their captors couldn't have anything but bad intentions for them. They were probably on their way to being sold into the sex trade.

Nora's heart squeezed hard in her chest. These children did not deserve the life their captors had in store for them. They deserved to be children, to run, to play and to learn to read and write and become responsible, productive citizens.

Nora would have considered jumping out of the back of the truck as it moved along the dusty road, but for two things.

One, the two scary guards sitting near the tailgate, rifles resting across their thighs.

Two, she couldn't abandon the children.

If there was any way to get them out of their

current situation, she had to try. For sure, she couldn't abandon them.

They drove for a very long time, dust kicking up behind them, filling the back of the truck, making Nora's throat dry and making her cough.

Nora held Taara in her lap.

The child lay with her head against Nora's breast, asleep in the dark and dust.

Even the armed men sitting with the children in the back of the truck nodded off several times.

At one point, Nora considered taking one of their guns and shooting them both. But the thought of missing, and the ensuing shooting match that might follow, made her rethink that option. She didn't want one of the children to be hit in the crossfire. And the truck would still be moving. How would she get the children off without injuring one or more of them? And injured, how would they find their way back to the base or to someone who would help them?

The long straight roads turned curvy, and the truck engine strained on an incline. By the feel and sound of the engine downshifting, they were heading into hills.

When they finally came to a stop, Nora jerked awake.

The men in the bed of the truck with them dropped down and started grabbing children. One of the men dropped a child. When the little girl hit the ground, she cried out in pain.

Nora lurched forward. "Stop! Don't hurt them! They're just children," she shouted. "I'll get them down."

The man grabbed her arm and yanked her off the truck without giving her a chance to get her feet beneath her. She landed on her side. Pain ripped through her hip and leg.

He jerked her up by the arm and dragged her toward the building. The only light she had to go by was from the headlights of the truck.

Nora looked back at the man tossing children to the ground.

Taara was lifted off the truck and dropped to the ground. She hit hard and fell to her knees.

Nora cried out and reached for her.

Taara struggled to her feet and ran after Nora, crying.

Nora fought to free her arm from her captor's grip. She shook loose and ran for the little girl.

She was brought up short when the man behind her grabbed her by her hair and yanked her backward. Nora landed hard on her bottom.

The man didn't give her the chance to get up, but dragged her the rest of the way into the building by her hair. Not until they were inside, did he let go and go back out to bring in more children.

Nora scrambled to her feet and ran for the door. A guard carrying an AK-47 stepped in front of her and yelled at her.

When Nora didn't stop, he yelled at her and thrust the butt of his weapon upward, hitting Nora in the gut.

She doubled over, the air knocked from her lungs, her belly hurting.

Taara was shoved through the door and fell to her knees.

Nora scooped her up into her arms.

The child buried her face against Nora's neck and sobbed.

"It's okay," Nora said. "It's okay." Although it wasn't okay. She didn't have a clue how she would get the children away from their kidnappers.

The little girls gathered around her, holding onto her legs, wrapping their arms around her waist and crying. They were terrified.

Frankly, Nora was terrified, too. But she couldn't show the children just how frightened she was. They needed someone to give them hope and support.

After all the little girls were shoved into the building, the men with the guns left, closing the door behind them.

Darkness surrounded them, engulfed them, seeming to swallow them alive.

For a moment, Nora's heart sank to her knees. How was she to get out of this place when she couldn't even see her hand in front of her face?

The children huddled closer.

Nora sat on what felt like hardpacked dirt and

ELLE JAMES

gathered the girls close. She stroked their heads, crooned to them and promised she would do her best to get them back to their home.

Deep down, she prayed for a miracle.

As she settled onto the dirt, with the girls all lying around her, sleep overtook her, claiming her in the darkness. Her last thought as she closed her eyes was of Rucker.

When his unit got back from their mission, would they come looking for her and the girls? Was one nurse and a group of Afghan orphans worthy of a major rescue attempt?

She really hoped so. The way things were looking, they could use all the help they could get.

RUCKER COULD HAVE KICKED himself for not giving Nora one of the GPS tracking devices they had plenty of. If she'd had one when the men had taken her, the Delta Force team would've been on their way immediately to retrieve her.

Instead, they waited to hear from Pazir. He had until morning to tell them something.

Rucker paced the operations room. His team-mates lay sleeping in their bunks, getting as much rest as they could after laying out all their gear. They could be ready to go in less than ten minutes from the time they were notified to saddle up.

Sleep wasn't in the cards for Rucker. Nora was

out there somewhere. If Akund had her, he was known for selling women and children into the sex trade. If that was their plan for Nora and the little girls, they only had a few hours to work with. Akund wouldn't sit on them long. He'd sell them and have them delivered as quickly as possible. Possibly to another country. Who knew where?

Another trip to the end of the room and back had Rucker working himself up into a frenzy.

If Pazir waited until morning to let them know where they were holding the hostages, it would be a very long night. And Nora could be that much farther away.

"You need to relax and kick your feet up," the CO said. "It's going to be a long night."

"Sir, I can't relax. Not while Nor—Lieutenant Michaels and those children are missing."

"You'll be of little use rescuing them if you're so tired you can't perform the mission."

"I know that, sir, but I just can't rest."

"The lieutenant is a remarkable woman, isn't she?" his commander said.

"Yes, sir. She is."

"I imagine she made an impression on you, what with delivering a breech baby and all."

So many things about the woman had impressed Rucker from the start. "Yes, sir. She's supposed to redeploy to the States in a couple of days. She should've stayed behind the wire for the entire last week of her tour."

"I understand she's to be admired for her commitment to the children. She risked her life to make sure they had the proper vaccinations to save their lives."

Rucker smiled. "She was determined to do that. I asked her to wait until we could escort her."

"But we had a Taliban leader to capture."

Rucker's lips pressed into a tight line. "Which we've failed to do now, twice."

"He's a slippery bastard. I feel like we're getting closer."

"Sir, close only counts with horseshoes and hand grenades." Rucker spun away and paced the length of the room then spun to face the CO. "Either we catch him, or we don't. The longer he's free, the more havoc he spreads. And if I find he's responsible for the capture of the little girls and Lieutenant Michaels, I will personally make him pay."

The commander nodded. "He needs to be eliminated one way or another."

A knock sounded on the door before a uniformed woman pushed it and poked her head inside. "Sir, I have a message for a Sergeant Sloan. The MP who brought it to me at the medical facility said the man who delivered it to the gate guard insisted it be passed to him as quickly as possible."

Rucker dove for the handwritten sheet of paper in her hand. "Thank you."

Lance entered the room after the female specialist left. "Hear anything?"

"Just got word." Rucker tore into the small envelope and removed the single sheet of paper with scrawling on it Rucker could barely read.

The message was written in spidery English.

Abdul Akund takes his product to one of two places to sell. One is in a small village in the Wardak Province. The other is in the heart of the hills west of Kabul. I leave you with the coordinates. Peace be with you.

Rucker fought the urge to crumple the paper and throw it across the room. Two places? He needed a definitive direction. Not two.

His commander read the note and handed it to Lance, the team computer guy. "Scan it and send it to the email address I have written on the pad beside the keyboard."

Lance scanned it into the computer and emailed the image to the address the CO indicated.

"I have people on standby at Langley," their commander said. "They'll pull up any satellite images they can at those coordinates and get back to us ASAP."

"Do we have to wait?" Rucker asked. "Can't we send men to both locations?"

"We could, but we only have one helicopter at our disposal at this time. It's all of the team or none."

Which meant more waiting.

Rucker had just about worn a path into the floor by the time Langley got back with them.

Lance sat at the desk with the computer, tapping a finger on the mouse, reading the latest news reports and studying the map of Afghanistan and where the coordinates fell.

Rucker stood at his side, wishing he could just get in a helicopter and go to both locations.

An hour passed and nothing.

Then Lance leaned forward. "Got something."

He tapped the mouse and brought up a satellite video of a building nestled in the hills with a truck parked beside it. Green heat signatures indicated people moving around outside of the building.

"Holy hell, look how little some of the heat signatures are."

"Children," Rucker said. "They're unloading children from the truck and moving them into that building." He spun and headed for the door. "Time to saddle up. We have our target. I'll gather the team."

"I'll notify the helicopter pilot," the commander said.

Rucker hurried to the buildings where his teammates slept, pounded on their doors and flung them open. "Moving out," he said as the men leaped out of their beds, strapped on their body armor and grabbed their weapons.

By the time the team assembled at the helicopter

pad, the pilot had the engine humming and the blades turning.

Rucker prayed they'd arrive in time to keep Akund from moving them, again.

Hang in there, Nora. The cavalry is on its way.

CHAPTER 10

AN HOUR INTO THE DARKNESS, the night cooled. Nora shrugged out of her uniform jacket and covered a couple of the little girls who couldn't quite make it close enough to her to share her body heat.

Most of them had fallen asleep, their little sobs breaking Nora's heart.

She wanted to make these men pay for being so callous with the lives of innocent children. Hadn't they been through enough after having lost their parents?

As she lay surrounded by little girls, a cool draft lifted the hairs that had worked free of the once neat bun at the nape of her neck. She brushed the hair aside and shivered in her T-shirt.

Then it hit her. Where there was a draft, there was an opening.

Nora untangled herself from the pile of children

and crawled along the floor in the direction she remembered the door was located.

When she bumped softly into the corrugated door, she sat up and ran her hands across the cool metal surface until she found the gap between the door and the wall. Running her fingers upward, she found where hinges held the door onto the side of the building. Those hinges were on the outside of the structure. She couldn't work them free. Cool air edged through the gaps but not enough to account for the breeze floating across the middle of the warehouse floor. Moving as quickly as possible, she worked her way to one corner, and started moving along the next wall.

Crawling along the floor, she searched for that breeze until she finally found it in the middle of the second wall. A gap between the floor and the wall caught the wind and funneled it into the room. It wasn't much of a gap, but the floor was dirt. With some effort, she might make it big enough to get the children through and, maybe, herself.

Using her fingernails, she scraped at the dirt. It was hardpacked and not moving quickly enough. What she needed was a tool of some kind. In her crawling, she hadn't run across anything she could use as a shovel. All she had was what she'd arrived in. Her uniform.

She patted down her pockets and found her ID card and dog tags. They weren't much, but they were better than nothing. Using her ID card, she scraped at the dirt, making little progress. Digging the corner of her card into the ground, she attempted to loosen larger chunks. The card bent. The ground was really hard.

Switching to her dog tags, she worked at the edges of the gap and slowly scraped dirt and dust away, shifting it to the side and spreading it out so that it wouldn't draw attention.

Hope grew with each inch she opened in the gap. Soon, she could get her arm through to the outside. The side she worked on was the side away from where the men had parked the vehicles. They shouldn't be paying as much attention to this side. Nora prayed she was right.

Time passed. An hour went by based on the dial on her watch. Still, she didn't have quite enough dirt removed to get the largest child through the opening. Definitely not enough to get herself through. She'd have to dig a lot more and faster if she planned to get out before sunup.

Engine noise sounded outside as if someone was driving up to the building.

Nora felt her way back across the floor and gathered the little girls around her. She'd just settled onto the floor when the big door opened, and a flashlight beam swept across her and the little girls.

She blinked, the light blinding her after being entombed in pitch black.

A man wearing the loose clothing of the Afghans and a black turban with a red-checkered band woven through it held the light. A taller man, wearing western trousers, a brown leather jacket and a wide-brimmed safari hat pulled down low over his face stepped in beside the Afghan.

"I didn't ask for adults," the man said in English with an American accent.

"She was with them when we collected them. It was take her or kill her. Her golden hair will bring top dollar."

"And the fact she's a missing soldier and a female one at that will have every military unit searching for her."

The man in the black turban raised his other hand. In it was a pistol. "We will hide the body."

Nora tensed and shoved Taara out of her arms. She crab-walked backward, away from the children and pushed to her feet.

The American placed his hand on the Afghan's arm. "No. I'll take her with the rest. But we have to move them quickly. I have a truck on its way. It will be here in the next hour."

"We would move them in our truck, but one of the tires is now flat. We are waiting for another to arrive before we can leave."

"No. I'd rather take them in my own transport, which will arrive soon. When it does, have them loaded quickly. The longer they remain here, the more chance there is of them being found."

When the flashlight beam started around the sides of the building, Nora tensed. She couldn't let them see the hole she'd worked so hard to dig. "You won't get away with this," she blurted.

The flashlight returned to her face, blinding her.

Nora held her hand up to block the light from reaching her eyes. "My unit will be looking for me. When they find me, your operation will be blown apart."

"You are one female," the man in the black turban said in heavily accented English. "They will not care."

The man with the hat shook his head. "They will," he disagreed. "Thus the need to move the assets quickly."

"We're not assets," Nora said. "We're not cattle, and we're not products to be bought or sold to the highest bidder. Not only is what you're doing against every law in the world, it's against humanity."

"If she doesn't shut up, you can stuff a rag in her mouth," the American said. "If she gives you any trouble, my people have drugs to handle her."

Nora's breath caught in her throat. She'd read the articles, seen the reports and knew how human trafficking worked.

They captured the women, drugged them into a stupor and used them until they were worn out or died of overdoses. The women didn't fight back because they couldn't. The drugs took the fight out of them and left them limp and lethargic.

If they got the drugs into her, she wouldn't have a chance of getting the little girls away from these monsters.

At that point, she prayed they'd leave her and the girls alone in the dark so that she could get back to work digging the way out of their prison. With less than an hour to work with, she had to get going.

The American glanced at her one more time, his eyes narrowing. "On second thought, if she gives you any trouble, you will be better off shooting her."

His words should've frightened Nora. But all they did was make her angry. So angry she wanted to succeed in her effort to break free of her captors and show them that she wasn't afraid, nor was she playing the part of a victim. Then she'd find the traitor American and...

Well, she hoped he'd rot in hell one way or another. He didn't deserve to live. Nor did the Afghan who'd gathered the victims to sell. They were lower than pond scum as far as Nora was concerned. Hell, pond scum had more redeeming qualities than those two men.

The men turned and left the building, taking the light with them.

As they left, Nora scanned the interior while there was still a little light left before they closed the door.

As she suspected, there wasn't any other tool she could use to dig the hole she needed to get out of the structure. After hugging the girls and telling them it would be all right, she found her way back to the hole she'd worked on and dropped to her knees. After a few minutes, one of the older girls crawled up to where she was and felt around for what she was doing.

Nora guided her hand to the hole in the floor like the blind leading the blind and showed her through her motions what she'd been working on.

She handed her the dog tags and went back to work on one side of the depression, digging deeper, as fast as she could, praying the ID card held up long enough to do the job.

The girl worked as hard on her side with the dog tags. It was like digging a trench with a spoon. It could be done, but it took time.

When her fingers started cramping and her knees went numb, she kept going. The girls needed her to get them out of there. She couldn't let a little pain stop her, so she dug deeper, calling on the last reserves of energy she could muster.

A sliver of starlight shone through the hole, growing bigger the more they dug.

As the light grew, the girls moved closer and helped by digging with their hands.

Nora and the older girl loosened the soil, the littler girls moved it out of the way.

Finally, Nora put out her hand to stop them all. She lay flat on her back and scooted under the wall. When she had her head out enough to see, she looked around.

As she'd suspected, there weren't any guards on that side of the building, but there was one at each corner. They'd have to be careful not to make too much noise or movement while the guards were looking their direction. Getting all the little girls past the guards would be risky, but then, staying in the building wasn't an option.

Nora slid back inside and dug faster and harder. She could literally see the light at the end of the tunnel, and she couldn't stop until she got the girls out.

Between her and the orphans, they dug the hole deep enough for Nora to get her head and shoulders through it. She came back inside and pressed a finger to her lips, hoping the children could see her in the little bit of light filtering inside the hut.

They nodded as one.

Nora pointed to the small children. "Little ones first."

Again, the kids nodded.

Nora poked her head beneath the wall and looked for the guards at the corners. One was in sight, with his back to the front wall and to her.

The other was nowhere to be seen.

She shimmied through the hole, almost getting

hung up when she got to her hips. Her belt caught the metal wall, making a clanking sound.

Nora lay still, watching the guard leaning against the wall up front. He didn't move, and his head appeared to be tipped toward his chest.

She hoped that meant he was asleep.

After she unhooked her belt from the wall, she wiggled and scooched and finally got her boots out as well.

She lay flat on the ground and very still until she was sure the other guard was still gone and the one on the front still slept. Then she reached back into the hole.

Little hands caught hers, and she pulled the first child through. It was Taara.

Nora almost cried in relief. She picked her up and carried her over to a stand of brush several yards away from the building. She sat her on the ground and pointed to her. "Stay here."

She wasn't sure Taara understood her words, but she hoped she would understand her meaning.

Then Nora looked both ways and ran back to the hole and reached inside.

One by one, she pulled the little girls free and hid them in the bushes.

She counted each one as she freed them and didn't stop until she had moved each child through the gap.

The older girl who'd helped her dig was the last

one through. She was halfway out when she heard the sound of engines and the loud clanking of the heavy metal door being opened.

Nora yanked the child through, grabbed her up in her arms and ran for the bushes. She set the child on her feet then knelt and slung one of the little girls up on her back to ride piggyback, then lifted two more up into her arms. The rest of the girls grabbed hands and followed Nora through the brush, moving quickly away from their prison and the men who would sell them like animals.

A shout sounded from the front of the building, echoing off the metal walls.

Nora moved faster. Their escape had been noted. She couldn't move too fast or she'd lose one of the girls. If they didn't move fast enough, they'd all be caught. They needed to keep going and get as much distance as possible between them and their captors.

She wasn't sure how far the little ones could go before they wore out and couldn't go a step further.

In the back of her mind, she hoped a knight in shining armor would appear and rescue them. Or a dozen knights in desert camouflage would swoop down from the sky in a Black Hawk helicopter and carry them away to safety. A girl had dreams.

CHAPTER 11

THE HELICOPTER SET them down on the other side of the ridge from the coordinates they'd been given. From there, the Delta Force Operatives moved to the top of the ridge, studied the terrain on the other side and still couldn't see their target. Based on the contour map they'd studied of the area, there was another hill they had to climb over to get to the building where they hoped to find the captives.

Not hoped...They *would* find Nora and the orphans.

The steep terrain slowed the team. Rucker took point, charging up the hills and down the ravines with more speed than finesse. Every second counted in this race.

As he rose to the top of the hill close to their destination, he slowed and eased up to the ridgeline, keeping low to the ground. He didn't want to present his silhouette as a target to whatever sentries they may have in place to guard their prizes. He also didn't know if they had a sniper positioned on the ridgeline he was easing up on. If so, he'd have to take him out first.

"What do you see?" Mac asked.

"Nothing yet," Rucker said. He had his night vision goggles pulled down over his eyes as he scanned the ridgeline in front of him. A bright green heat signature glowed at the top, half hidden in the underbrush.

They had a gunman in position to provide cover for their men below and to alert them if someone was coming up the road.

Apparently, they didn't expect anyone to come across the rugged hills behind them.

That was their first mistake.

"One bogey on the ridge. Moving in."

"I've got your six," Dash said. "Coming up on your right rear."

Rucker eased upward, carefully placing his feet to keep from disturbing loose rocks and alerting his target of his approach.

The man didn't even know he was being stalked until too late.

"Sniper eliminated," Rucker reported. "All clear on the ridge."

The team moved upward as Rucker studied the building below. "I count six bogeys that I can see.

One on each corner, two standing near a truck parked at the side and another leaning against the door on the front of the building."

"See any sign of the kids or your nurse?" Dash asked.

"She's not my nurse," Rucker insisted. "And no to both."

Headlights flashed on a zigzagging road below, leading up to the metal building. A truck approached and pulled to a stop in front of the building.

The guard at the door turned and opened the door. A man carrying a flashlight stepped inside. A moment later, he came out shouting in what sounded like Pashto.

The guards on the corners ran to the front to see what was the matter.

"Someone isn't happy down there," Dash said. "I have a feeling they've misplaced whatever was supposed to be in that building."

Rucker cursed softly. "Are we too late?"

"The only way to know is to get down and find out for ourselves," Dash said as he came up behind Rucker. "Your nurse is pretty smart. If there was a way to get those kids out of there, she would've found it."

Rucker nodded. "We'd better hurry. Looks like reinforcements are on their way up the hill. We need to get to their escapees before those vehicles arrive."

The Deltas spread out and slipped over the ridge.

Then they half-ran, half-slid down the steep slope to the back and side of the building away from the lights of the trucks.

The noise of the shouts helped to cover the sounds they made descending the hill to where the structure stood. It looked as if someone had built it recently.

Rucker's lips pressed into a thin line. If this was one of Akund's transfer stations for his human trafficking, the money must be good in the market of selling people.

The bastard needed to die. Rucker hoped they'd find him there so that he could be the one to take him down.

As they neared the building, Rucker went around the side away from the one where the truck was parked. As he ran hunkered low, starlight glinted off something shiny. He slowed and reached down to pick it up.

His heart skipped several beats. He held a single metal dog tag in his hand. In the light from the stars above, he could read the name on it.

Michaels, Nora

He looked at the ground again and noticed it dipped down into the side of the metal building where a shallow tunnel had been dug out of the dirt.

"She got them out," Rucker whispered into his mic and looked to the brush several yards from the building.

The beam of a flashlight shined through the tunnel, and a man's voice echoed off the walls inside the structure.

"I'm going after them," Rucker said, heading for the brush.

"You and the rest of these yahoos," Dash said.

Rucker ducked low as he ran away from the men and the building, hoping he was running in the same direction Nora and the children had gone. He had to get to them before Akund's men found them. They might decide to shoot rather than recapture them. Especially the adult who'd gotten them out right under their noses.

If Akund wasn't there, these men were in jeopardy of the Taliban leader's wrath for losing the product that would pay for the man's next expensive SUV or the weapons he would employ against NATO forces.

Yeah, they'd be pretty desperate to find Nora and the orphans. But not as desperate as Rucker. He had to get to them first and provide some kind of protection to keep them safe.

"Go," Dash said. "We're coming up behind Akund's men. We'll do what we can to keep them from catching up to you and the children."

Rucker settled his night vision goggles down over his eyes and scanned the terrain ahead. At first, he could see nothing but brush and hills. Then as he looked again, he spotted a faint green heat signature in the distance, running down into a ravine. It wasn't an animal but a human, running upright and too big to be a child.

He chased after it.

Men shouted behind him, crashing through the underbrush, heading in Rucker's direction.

"Could use a little support about now," he murmured as he ran after the silhouette he hoped would be Nora. It was a single figure, making him wonder if it was her at all. Where were the children? Had they already been moved, leaving Nora behind? Was he racing after someone other than Nora? If so…who?

With the enemy behind him and the hope of Nora in front of him, Rucker kept running.

As he grew closer to the figure ahead of him, he could tell by its shape and the way it ran it was a female.

It had to be Nora. But where were the children?

"Got a couple of truckloads and a moving van headed up the hill," Dawg reported. As originally planned, their best sniper had chosen a position overlooking their target location. "It appears there are two big trucks headed this way, loaded to the max with men and guns. I'm guessing about two dozen. We'll want to deal with the few we have and bug out before the rest arrive."

"How long do we have?" Dash asked.

"Five minutes tops," Dawg responded.

"I'm following the lieutenant," Rucker said. "I'm betting she's stashed the kids somewhere close. Find them. Airlift them out of here while the lieutenant and I create a distraction."

"Roger," Dash said.

As Rucker drew closer to the green blob in his night vision goggles, the silhouette grew more distinctive—it was definitely a woman running ahead of him.

"Nora!" he called out, afraid he'd alert the men following him to his location, but more afraid Nora would fall over the edge of a cliff before he caught up with her.

Ahead of him, she fell.

Rucker pushed harder, taking advantage of her fall to catch up.

She scrambled to her feet and took off again.

He caught her arm and spun her to face him. "Let go of me!" she yelled and pounded his chest.

"Nora." Rucker wrapped his arms around her, trapping her hands between them. "It's me, Rucker. Stop fighting. We don't have time for this."

She looked up, starlight glinting off her eyes. "Rucker. Oh, sweet Jesus." Her body went slack, her chest heaving to fill her starving lungs.

"Sweetheart, we don't have time. We have to keep running."

"I can't. I just can't," she said, sagging against him and resting her forehead on his chest.

"We have to. There are men behind me."

As if on cue, a shot rang out.

Nora's head jerked, and she turned to run.

Rucker pulled her over the edge of a hill and pushed her to the ground. Below them he could see the winding road leading up to the building in the hills. The two trucks Dawg had mentioned were halfway up the winding road.

"See those trucks?" he whispered.

"I do. Are they ours?"

"No," Rucker said. "The first two are filled with Taliban. We have to slow them down while my guys find the children and get them out by chopper."

"What about the men following us?"

"We're about to take care of them," Rucker said as he poked his head above the ridgeline, fitted his night vision goggles in place and identified the men heading his direction.

"I have three bogeys in sight, approximately twenty yards from my current position. Tell me it's not any of you," he said into his mic.

"Blade, Bull, Dawg and I are still back by the building," Mac said. "We took out four guys standing around the truck."

"Tank and I will clean up the two slackers chasing after you," Dash said. "Can you manage the three closing in on you?"

"Will do," Rucker said. "Then we're heading down to the road to slow the arrival of their reinforcements. Find those kids and get them out ASAP."

"I left them hidden in a big ravine behind the building," Nora said.

"Look in the big ravine behind the building," Rucker said into his mic.

"Roger," Dash said.

Rucker studied the three men, not far from each other, moving through the brush in their direction.

He waited until he had them close enough he couldn't miss. With three of them, his aim had to be true and fast in order to take them out before they dropped to the ground to hide.

He zeroed in on the closest man. They all moved slowly, having lost sight of their quarry.

Rucker stared through his sight, squeezed the trigger and shifted to the second man quickly, squeezing off the next round.

The third guy dropped to his knees.

From Rucker's position on the ridge, he was slightly above the man and could see him clearly.

He fired again, and the man fell the rest of the way to the ground.

With little time to spare, Rucker turned, grabbed Nora's hand and shouted, "Move!"

They half-ran, half-slipped down the hill moving toward a position in the road below he hoped to arrive at before the two trucks did.

They had seconds to get close enough to make a difference.

One more rise, one more ravine, and they'd be there.

As they passed over the rise and dropped down into the ravine, Rucker grabbed Nora's arm. "Ever thrown a baseball?" he asked.

"I was on the softball team in high school," she said.

He grinned. "How about a grenade?"

"Once during leadership training, but it was just a dummy grenade," she said. "Why?"

He plucked a grenade from his vest and handed it to her. "You remember how to use this?"

She nodded with her eyes wide. "Yes."

"This is important," he said. "When we get up to that road, I'm going to throw mine at the first truck. You will throw at the second. All you have to do is get it close to the wheels. Disable the truck, and that will slow them down enough for the helicopter to get in, load the children and get out. Got it?"

She nodded, still looking scared but her jaw firming. "We have to give them time to get those girls to safety."

"Right." He captured her cheeks between his hands and kissed her hard. "You're amazing, Lieutenant Michaels. Abso-fuckin-lutely amazing." He grabbed her free hand and helped her out of the ravine.

They ran toward the road. When they were within fifty feet, Rucker pointed to a boulder. "Get behind that. Once you throw, duck low, hands over your ears and wait for the bang."

Nora dropped down below the boulder, holding the grenade in her hand.

Rucker ran a little farther up the hill and dropped behind another boulder.

Seconds later, the first truck rounded the curve in the road and lumbered toward them.

The second truck wasn't very far behind.

Rucker waited until the truck was within a few feet of his target. He pulled the ring, counted to two and lobbed the grenade at the truck's wheels.

After a quick glance in Nora's direction to witness her most excellent throw, he ducked behind the boulder, pressed his hands over his ears and closed his eyes.

The first grenade went off with a loud bang, shaking the ground beneath Rucker.

Two seconds later, the second one went off.

Rucker didn't wait for the dust to clear. He ran to where Nora was hiding behind the boulder, grabbed her hand and took off for the ravine.

Shouts behind them made him run faster.

Nora kept up, leaping over rocks, brush and anything in the way of their goal.

As they scrambled down the steep sides of the ravine, gunfire sounded over their heads.

Rucker kept Nora moving, traveling down the hill, away from the extraction operation above. Hopefully, the men in the backs of the trucks would be more interested in chasing them than continuing up to the building to surprise the helicopter lifting the children out of the hills.

"Found the girls. Loading them into the helicopter as we speak," Dash reported. "Might have to make two trips to get all of us out."

"Can't," Rucker said. "Get all of them out of there. I'll get the lieutenant to somewhere safe."

"We're not leaving without you," Dash said.

"You have to," Rucker said as he leaped over a crevice. "There are too many of these guys down here. We can't risk the girls being caught in the crossfire."

"What about you and the lieutenant?" Bull asked.

Struggling to hear what they were saying, breathe and get the hell away from the men they'd just pissed off, Rucker barked into his mic, "We'll get as far from here as possible. I have the GPS tracker the CO gave us, you can come back when you've delivered the children to someplace safe."

"Roger," Bull said. "Good luck."

They'd need a lot more than good luck to outrun the men from those trucks.

As they reached the base of the hills, Nora stumbled and fell to her knees. She was tired, bruised and breathing so hard she couldn't stand up straight.

Shouts from above indicated the men from the trucks were still on their tails.

A vehicle roared along the road, heading toward them at extreme speed.

Nora and Rucker's instincts had them turn back toward the hills from which they'd just emerged.

The vehicle, a battered, older model small pickup rumbled to a stop, and a man got out, wielding an AK-47.

They didn't have time to run for cover. If this man intended to kill them, he could already have done so.

"Lieutenant Michaels? Sergeant Sloan?" the man called out.

Rucker recognized the voice, and his eyes narrowed. "Pazir?"

"Come quickly," he urged.

Taking a leap of faith, Rucker hooked Nora's arm and ran toward the truck and Pazir.

The truck was small, too small to fit them both into the front seat with Pazir.

"In the back," he motioned toward the bed of the truck filled with boxes, junk and a blanket.

Rucker helped Nora into the back as Pazir slipped into the driver's seat and set the truck in motion. Running alongside the truck, Rucker leaped up onto the rim of the bed and rolled in, landing on top of Nora.

For a long moment, he lay with his entire body pressed the length of hers.

A particularly harsh bump reminded him where they were. If that wasn't enough, the shots fired as they retreated brought him back to his senses.

"Rucker, you two gonna make it?" Dash's voice came over his mic, the static making it almost unintelligible.

"We got a ride out of the hot zone. You got the girls?"

"We got all of them," Dash said. "On our way up and out."

"I'll get word to you about how to collect us. Might be tricky."

Rucker glanced toward the hilltop as the Black Hawk helicopter rose into the sky.

The men emerging at the bottom of the hill aimed their rifles at the truck until they saw and heard the helicopter as it banked and flew away from the Taliban and their cruel intentions for a bunch of little girls.

Once they figured their bullets would have no impact on the chopper, the gunmen turned their weapons on the truck speeding down the dirt road.

They were far enough away their bullets fell short. In the distance, Rucker could see the enclosed moving truck emerge from the mountain road onto the main dirt road Pazir was traveling. They were being followed. The truck must have been heavier and slower because the distance between them lengthened until Rucker couldn't see any headlights.

Alone on the road, Rucker lay back amid the junk and boxes, slipped his arm behind Nora and pulled her close.

"The girls are going to be all right," he said. "They got them out."

Nora stretched her arm across his middle and buried her face against his chest. "Thank you."

They rode like that for what felt like hours, the bumps in the road creating bruises on Rucker's body. He didn't care. For the moment, he had Nora in his arms. To hell with regulations. He needed to feel her, touch her and hold her, knowing she was alive and safe for the moment.

When they returned to the base, he'd have to go back to the real world and the fact that he couldn't act on the feelings growing inside him.

For a man who'd sworn to remain a bachelor for his entire career in the Army, he now knew the error of that kind of thinking. He wanted what other men had...a partner in life. One who was his equal, who could hold her own and stand beside him through good times and bad, through deployments and uncertainty.

Hell, he was falling in love with Nora. If he pursued her, he could ruin her military career. If he didn't, he might regret letting her go for the rest of his life.

CHAPTER 12

Nora fell asleep in Rucker's arms, exhausted from digging the hole that had freed her and the kids, drained by the fear and worry that they wouldn't get away from their captives alive.

The back of the truck was hard on her backside, but it was a hell of a lot better than being drugged and used as a sex toy by creepy, horrible men who paid for sex with children and comatose women.

Pazir drove through the night, slowing only as he entered and left small villages along the road. While it was still dark, and before the gray light of morning spread across the eastern horizon, the defecting member of the Taliban came to a stop outside a town of a couple hundred mud and stick homes.

He got out of the truck and came around to the bed. "You must cover up. No one must know you are with me."

Rucker grabbed one of the blankets he'd been using as a pillow and spread it over his and Nora's bodies. When that wasn't quite enough, he used a second one and finished the job, leaving his head out long enough to talk to Pazir.

"Thank you for coming to our rescue. How did you know we'd need help?"

"I have people everywhere." He held up a cellphone. "We are not all current on technology, and sometimes, we do not have reception, but we can communicate. I got a text that Akund had a sale scheduled immediately and knew his buyer would come heavily armed."

"You saved our lives," Nora said. "You don't owe us a life debt anymore."

Pazir dipped his head once. "I cannot consider my debt repaid until you are with your people back at the base." The corners of his lips twitched. "My wife insisted my debt would not be done until then."

"Please, thank your wife for us," Nora said. "How is the baby?"

Pazir's grin started slowly and spread quickly across his face. "He is an amazing son. He will be a great leader someday."

"Has he had any problems nursing?" Nora asked.

"None." Pazir puffed out his chest and patted his belly. "His mother feeds him at all hours of the day and night. He has his father's appetite."

Nora smiled. "To be expected for a newborn. I'm

glad he's doing well. He had such a difficult beginning."

Pazir nodded, his face solemn. "Thanks to you both and the will of Allah, he is alive and doing well.

"Now, if you are ready, this is the town where we will stop. It is our new home. My wife's sister lives here. She has agreed to help us. An educated woman, she has no love of the Taliban." He nodded toward the blanket. "Until we are safe inside the walls of her home, please remain covered."

"We will," Rucker said.

Nora huddled beneath the blanket, not liking that she couldn't see. She had to hold on to her trust in Pazir to do right by them. He'd saved them from Akund once, surely he wouldn't turn the Americans over to the Taliban now.

The truck lurched forward.

Nora could tell they were moving slowly through a town by the way the truck slowed, sped up and slowed again. A dog barked somewhere but other than that, few other sounds came to her.

Finally, the truck slowed and turned. The creaking of a gate hinge sounded. The truck moved forward a few feet, and the same creaking sounded again followed by a clank as a gate latch clicked into place.

For another long moment, Nora lay still beneath the blanket, lying beside Rucker, not in his arms. He needed those free to fire his weapon if the need arose. He had his handgun in his grip, ready if he was forced to come up fighting.

"You can come with me," Pazir's voice spoke softly over the side of the pickup.

Rucker tossed aside the blanket, sat up with his gun at the ready and looked around.

"Hurry and be quiet." Pazir waved his hand, urging them to follow. "The sun rises soon. No one must see you, or my family will be in grave danger."

Rucker nodded and rolled his body over the side of the truck to the ground. He helped Nora to the ground, hooked her arm in his grasp and followed Pazir into the home.

The door opened into a living area with a single candle burning on a table in the corner. A rug covered the floor and cushions lined the walls.

Pazir passed through the room and entered a long dark hallway.

A woman emerged from one of the rooms, carrying a baby and a candle. She spoke softly in Pashto.

Pazir answered.

The woman stepped aside, allowing Rucker and Nora to enter the room.

Inside, a pallet had been made up on the floor with a thin blanket and a pillow. The room had a small window, but a cloth had been hung over it, blocking any light shining in or out.

"You will stay here until it is safe to move you. Now, I will hide the truck."

"Is the truck yours?" Rucker asked.

Pazir shook his head. "It is one a cousin has been working on for some time to rebuild the engine and sell it. He will take it to another town in the night and sell it."

Nora worried that the Taliban could trace the truck to Pazir and his family. "Let me buy it. I will get the money to him, but he must take the truck to another town and leave it on the street. If there is no transaction recorded or remembered, no one will be able to trace it back to you or your cousin."

"How much does a truck like that cost?" Rucker asked.

Pazir named the price in Afghan currency.

Nora made a quick calculation in her head. "I have that. It will take me time to get it in cash."

Pazir nodded. "I will work with my cousin to have the truck taken to another town and left in the street with the keys in it."

Nora drew in a deep breath and let it out slowly. "We don't want to cause any trouble for you or your family."

Rucker nodded. "Thank you for helping us."

"I have my people watching our home and the streets for any sign of Taliban arrival. For now, you can sleep."

"Thank you," Nora said. Though the thought of even closing her eyes for a moment scared her, she knew she had to get enough sleep to restore some of her energy.

"My wife will serve food in the morning."

As if on cue, his wife appeared behind him and whispered to him. She pressed something into Pazir's hand.

He nodded and murmured back to her.

She left him and hurried down the hallway.

Pazir held out his hand. "My wife offers you bread to eat now until she cooks in the morning."

He handed Rucker two pieces of the flat bread common in the country.

Rucker accepted the offering. "Thank you."

Too hungry to refuse the offering, Nora smiled. "Thank you for your generosity. And please thank your wife for her concern."

Pazir bowed slightly and left the room, closing the door behind him and taking all light with him.

For a moment, Nora stood still, hoping her vision would adjust to the darkness.

A soft click sounded, and a red flashlight beam provided a soft glow, lighting the room just enough they wouldn't run into walls.

Rucker balanced a very small flashlight in one hand and stared down at the bread in the other hand. "These people have gone above and beyond to help us. If the Taliban learn they assisted us in our escape, they will be murdered as an example to others." He held out the bread. "Here, you take it."

"We both need to keep up our strength. We don't know if we'll be running out of here anytime soon."

Rucker nodded. "True. But I bet I've eaten more recently than you. Here." He took her hand and placed the flat bread in her palm.

Nora accepted the food and tore off a piece with her teeth. It had little taste, but she appreciated every bite as she paced the small room, consuming the bread. Pace might have been an overstatement of what she did. She took only two steps before bumping into Rucker.

After Nora had made five round trips, Rucker laid the flashlight on the floor, then hooked her arm and brought her up short. "Like food, your body needs rest to recuperate and rebuild energy."

She nodded. "Yeah. I realize that. I just wish we could do something. I want to know the girls made it back. Are they okay? Did any of them get hurt? Were any of your people harmed during the mission?" She tipped back her head and let go of a sharp stream of air. "I feel almost as trapped here as I did in that building on the hill. The only difference is that I have you and a flashlight." She laughed softly and raised her dirty hands. "And I hope I don't have to dig my way out of here."

He raised her dirty hands to his lips and kissed her fingertips. "Your hands are beautiful. What you did for the children was amazing. I was scared for you and the girls. Those men are known for their ruthlessness." He cupped her cheek. "I know it's against all the rules, and I could be court-marshalled, but I want to kiss you so bad, I'd risk everything."

Nora's heart pounded against her ribs, and her breathing became erratic. Her gaze shifted from his eyes to his lips. She wanted to kiss him and knew it was wrong, but after all that had happened that day, she couldn't deny herself.

She rose up on her toes, meeting his lips with her own. Her hands slipped up his chest to wrap around the back of his neck, and she pulled him closer, opening to him.

Rucker's arms came up around her, pulling her close, their hips meeting, the hard evidence of his desire pressing into her belly, making her want him even more.

His tongue pushed inside to claim hers, sweeping the length and back, caressing her in a way she'd never felt before. Yes, she'd been kissed and had sex before, but the way he commanded her mouth, yet gave her the option to end it at any time, made it all that much more poignant.

God, she wanted him. Just when she reached for the buttons on his uniform jacket, a soft knock sounded on the door.

Nora sprang back and smoothed the loose hairs around her face back behind her ears.

Rucker opened the door to Gulpari, the new mother.

The woman carried a jug of water and a large bowl. She set them on the ground, laid a square of fabric and a cake of soap beside it and bowed out of the room, closing the door.

Nora smiled. "I was wondering when I'd ever feel clean again." She nodded to the water. "Do you want to go first? My hands alone will make the water muddy."

"No, you go first." He sat on the pallet on the floor and watched as she poured water into the bowl.

Knowing he was watching and still feeling the effects of the kiss, Nora sat on the floor in front of the bowl, dipped the bar of soap in the water and created a head of suds. Then she washed her hands, working at getting the dirt out from beneath her frayed fingernails. When she was satisfied with her hands, she splashed water on her face and scrubbed behind her ears and down her neck. Then she reached for the hem of her T-shirt and slowly drew it up over her torso past her shoulders and off.

She knew what she was starting. Knew it was against all the rules and knew she could get in so much trouble if anyone found out.

When she reached for the hooks on her bra, callused hands brushed hers aside and worked them free. Those same hands brushed the straps down her arms, letting the garment fall to her waist.

Rucker's lips caressed the curve of her neck, his hands skimming over her shoulders and down her arms. "Tell me to stop...and I will," he whispered against her ear.

"Tell me you want this, that my rank isn't influencing your desire," she said, her breath catching and holding in her throat as she waited for his response.

He laughed. "If anything, your rank puts a damper on my desire. But not enough to make me want to stop." Again, he caressed the curve of her neck with his lips, brushing across the skin in a light, teasing motion.

Nora leaned backward and rested her head against his chest. "I've wanted this since the day you sat across the table drinking coffee with me. Is that crazy?"

"No crazier than me wanting you when we played volleyball in the sand," he murmured against her hair.

She laughed. "I was all hot and sweaty."

"More like hot and sexy. Your body was made for motion. You attacked the ball like you meant it and followed through. Still, you were a team player and didn't try to hog the court or the ball. And your legs...I could go on forever about your legs."

She reached up behind her and circled the back of his neck. "Why here? Why now? Why am I attracted to someone I can't have on the eve of redeploying back to the states?"

"Fate?" he said. "I had no intention of ever having

a long-term relationship. My job doesn't allow for it. Yet here I am, wishing we had a future. If for nothing else so that we could go out to eat at a restaurant, or see a movie, grab a beer or some barbeque."

She chuckled while turning to face him. "I like barbeque."

"I'm glad, because that's a deal breaker."

"Really? What if I was a vegetarian?" She pressed her naked breasts against his uniform jacket, feeling a little self-conscious about her state of undress and his fully clothed body. Reaching for the Velcro on his armored vest, she struggled to get the first strap free.

Again, he brushed aside her hands and made quick work of shedding the vest and then the shirt beneath it. When he was down to his T-shirt, Nora took over tugging it free of his trousers and dragging it up his torso and off.

He pulled her into his arms, holding her close so that they were skin to skin, the warm, red glow of the flashlight making the room even more intimate.

Then he set her at arm's length and lathered the soap, washing his hands, face, arms and chest, splashing water over himself to rinse.

Nora did the same and then used the towel to dry his skin. He took the towel from her and dried her. Then he wrapped his arms around her and laid back on the pallet with her.

For a long moment, he stared into her eyes, and

she stared into his. The desire she felt was mirrored in the dark depths of his irises.

She touched his face, her hand skimming over the rough stubble of his beard. Continuing her exploration, she trailed her hand down his neck, stopping to thumb the beat of his pulse at the base. Then she feathered her fingers across his broad shoulders and down his bulging biceps.

Feeling brave, she cut across his chest and tweaked the hard, brown nipples then bent to take one between her teeth, nipping it gently.

"Hey," he said. "Those are attached." He rolled her onto her back and pinned her wrists to the pallet on either side of her head. "Two can play this game."

"Glad to hear that. I thought I was going to have to take charge of this—"

He covered her mouth with his and kissed her slowly, teasing her tongue in a slow, sensuous caress.

Letting go of her wrists, he blazed a trail down the side of her jaw to capture her earlobe between his teeth for a playful nip. Not dwelling on any one place too long, he slipped lower, tonguing and nipping the skin along the long line of her neck to the base of her throat where her pulse beat wildly.

Already, her blood burned through her veins. Her nerves were on fire, every touch of his hands and lips sent electric shocks throughout her system, coiling low in her belly. Yes, this was what she'd wanted. What she needed now more than she needed a career in the Army. Hell, more than she needed to take her next breath. The way he was going, he'd have her begging him to take her. To hell with regulations.

One at a time, he captured her breasts in his mouth, sucking gently, tapping the nipples with the tip of his tongue, and then rolling the beaded tip between his teeth.

Nora's back arched off the ground, urging him to take more. "Please," she begged, not at all surprised he had her at that point already. He was taking it slow, building the tension, allowing her to adjust to what was happening.

"Too slow," she murmured.

He chuckled. "I want you to get there."

"I'm well on my way, and we aren't even naked yet," she said through clenched teeth, her breathing coming in ragged gasps. "Please, don't make me wait forever."

Rucker chuckled. "Almost. There." He abandoned her breasts and kissed every rib, dipping his tongue into her bellybutton and coming to a stop at the waistband of her uniform trousers.

With very slow and deliberate moves, he unbuttoned her pants and slipped his hand inside to cup her sex.

"Mmmm. Already wet," he noted.

When he took his hand out of her panties, she almost cried.

Then he was at her feet, unlacing her boots and

pulling them off, then drawing off her socks and tucking them into her boots. Within seconds, he had her trousers and panties off, and she lay naked on the pallet of colorful blankets, feeling gloriously sexy, even though she'd been running through the hills and throwing hand grenades. Nothing said sexy like pulling the pin on a hand grenade, right?

Rucker took a few moments to remove his boots and socks and unbutton his pants. He rose to his feet and stood over her to shuck his black trousers and boxer briefs.

Nora's gaze swept him from his eyes to his toes. Not one part of him disappointed. He was a study of beautiful masculinity with his firm, well-defined muscles, taut abs and his magnificent erection.

Nora smiled up at him. "What are the chances, a Delta Force guy carries a condom in his pocket to the field?"

He grinned. "I can't vouch for my teammates, but I carry a survival kit with me everywhere." He bent to retrieve his trousers, dug his hand into one of the cargo pockets and fished out a slim, credit-card-sized pouch. From it, he pulled out a WWII P-38 can opener, fishhook, razorblade, needle and thread and one foil-packaged condom.

"I get the feeling you were a Boy Scout some-where down the line."

"If by Boy Scout, you mean a horny little bastard,

you would be correct. However, I've never used this particular item of my survival kit."

"Until now." She reached for his hand and drew him down to her. "I hope it doesn't have an expiration date on it."

"Me, too," he said and kissed her, long and hard.

Nora wrapped her calf around the back of his leg, raising it up to clench around his thigh.

"Hold that thought. We're not done yet," he said. "I want you as hot and ready as I am."

"Oh, baby, I'm there," she moaned.

"Nope," he said and scooted down her body, performing a mini version of the foreplay he'd exhibited on her body up until then. When he reached the juncture of her thighs, he slowed the assault on her senses and spread open her thighs.

Nora's breath caught and held as Rucker parted her folds and bent to touch her clit with the tip of his tongue.

Her back arching off the ground, Nora swallowed the cry of pleasure rising up her throat. The man knew exactly what pleasure center to tap to make her entire body light up like a Roman candle.

When he flicked it again, she grabbed for his hair and threaded her fingers into the short strands.

Her senses pulled tight like the string on a guitar, there to be plucked and strummed by a master player.

And Rucker was the one, playing her like a master.

He swirled his finger around her opening

When he licked her there again, she jettisoned to the top of a giant wave of sensations. She rode it all the way back to shore, her body thrumming with her release.

If she'd hoped making love with Rucker would get him out of her system, she was completely wrong.

She grabbed him by the hair and urged him upward. If anything, she wanted him more than ever, seriously doubting she could ever get enough of this brave, Delta Force soldier.

CHAPTER 13

Rucker climbed up Nora's body and kissed her.

Her body writhed against his, still in the throes of passion.

Leaning up on one arm, he tore open the little foil packet.

Nora took it from him and rolled the condom over his hard shaft all the way to the base. For a few moments she fondled him before she guided him to her entrance.

He poised there, the tip of his cock barely touching the slick channel. Gathering his control, he slipped into her, slowly filling her.

Her hands rose to cup his ass, her fingers warm against his naked skin, increasing their pressure, urging him deeper.

Once he was all the way seated inside her, he gave

her time to adjust to his girth, letting her stretch to accommodate him.

Calling on every ounce of control he could muster, he moved slowly in and out, not wanting to hurt her.

Her fingers dug into his flesh, urging him to go faster, setting the pace to a swift steady rhythm.

Rucker liked the way she wrapped around him, how wet and warm she was and how she wanted him to go faster and faster.

She raised her knees, planting her heels into the ground, lifting her hips to meet him thrust for thrust.

The more he pumped and the faster he went, the tighter his body grew until he burst through the ceiling of his control and shot his release. One final thrust and he buried himself deep inside her velvety softness.

Her fingers squeezed, released and squeezed again until she drew in a deep breath and let it go in a long sigh. "Wow."

When he could breathe again, he chuckled. "Wow?"

"Uh huh," she said with a sleepy, satisfied smile. "That's all I have. Words can't convey the depth of what I'm feeling at this moment."

He dropped down on her and kissed her, then rolled onto his side, taking her with him.

Nora nestled her head into the crook of his shoulder, a hand resting on his chest. "I should really feel guilty or regretful for making love with you...but I just can't."

"No regrets here," Rucker admitted. "Unless what we've done gets you in trouble in any way. Then I'll only regret that it got you in trouble. I could never regret loving you." As soon as the word loving came out of his mouth, he realized what he'd just said. *Loving you.* Was that what this was?

Love?

For a man who'd sworn off falling in love, he was tumbling down that rabbit hole so fast he couldn't keep it from happening.

This woman. This amazing nurse and compassionate human being had stolen his heart. After everything that had happened...after tonight, how could he let her walk away?

He held her close while he could, unsure of what the next day would bring. Eventually, they'd have to go back to the base and back to being the officer she was and the enlisted man he was. "We really are between a rock and a hard place, aren't we?"

She closed her eyes and nodded, her cheek rubbing against his chest. "Pazir has gone so far to protect us, he's really put himself and his family in a bad place."

"I wasn't talking about Pazir and getting out of here without the Taliban finding out it was Pazir who picked us up on the road."

She twirled her finger around his nipple. "I know.

But getting away from the Taliban seems to be a whole lot easier than working anything out between you and me. I'd rather not think about it right now. I've dealt with enough trauma for one day." Nora yawned. "What was it you said about rest being another way to recuperate and rebuild our stores of energy?"

He laughed. "Is that what I said?"

"Yup." She yawned again. "I'm going to take your advice."

"About time," he said, smoothing the hair back from her face. "Sleep, sweetheart. We'll figure things out in the morning."

She leaned her head up. "Are goodnight kisses too old-fashioned?" she whispered.

"Goodnight kisses never go out of style," Rucker said and sealed her lips with his.

"That's good, because I could never get tired of them." She kissed him again, laid her cheek against his chest and closed her eyes. In less than a minute, she slept.

Rucker lay for a long time, loving the feel of her in his arms, the way her naked skin felt against his, the warmth of her breath on him.

Why did what they had between them have to be so complicated?

He knew he couldn't go to sleep without getting dressed. They would need to be ready to go in a flash should the Taliban come knocking on Pazir's door.

Yet, he lay for a long time, stocking up on memories of his time with Nora of how she'd made love passionately and with abandon. How she felt beside him.

Somehow, he had to make it work between them. This night together was only the beginning of something great and beautiful. He refused to let it be the beginning and the end wrapped up in one night's passion.

As the gray light of morning lightened the covered window, he rose, dressed, pulled on his boots, his bulletproof vest and pressed his radio communication earbuds into his ears. If his people chose to find him before he called for extraction, he wanted to know they were there.

He woke Nora with a kiss. "Hey, you might want to get dressed before Gulpari shows up with breakfast."

Nora rubbed her eyes, pushed up on her elbows and blinked. "What? Where am I ?"

"Good question," Rucker said. "We need to ask that one when we see Pazir."

"How will we get word to your guys for a pick-up?" she asked, slipping her arms into her bra.

Rucker had thought about that all night. His radio headset was short range. What he needed was a phone. But he couldn't use anything Pazir might have without leaving traces of his connection to the base and the people who were rescued by a lone driver in a beat-up truck.

They needed to get to a larger town with an electronics store where they might find a burner phone.

Nora pulled her T-shirt over her head and stood to dress in her uniform trousers. She had just laced her last boot when Gulpari burst through the door, carrying a bundle of clothing. She pressed a finger to her lips and pointed to the window.

Rucker's pulse leaped. "Taliban?" he whispered.

Gulpari nodded, crossed to the window and ripped the covering off. It was small, but they could fit through it.

Pazir's wife shoved the bundle she carried into Nora's arms. It contained what appeared to be two blue burqas that would cover them completely from head to toe. "You must go. Quickly."

"You'll have a harder time of it fitting through," Nora said. "You should go first."

When Rucker opened his mouth to disagree, Nora held up her hand. "No time to argue. Just go." Already, she was dragging one of the blue burqas over her head.

Rucker wasn't happy about going first. It left Nora at the mercy of whatever men were at Pazir's door.

He shoved his rifle through the opening and dropped it quietly to the ground. Then he pulled himself up through the small window, squeezing his shoulders through first. Next, he dropped down headfirst to the ground, catching himself with his arms.

Pazir's wife shoved the other burqa through the window after Rucker. It landed on the ground beside him.

The male voices near the front of the home grew louder. A door banged open, and the voices moved into the home.

"Nora," Rucker whispered through the window. "Hurry."

"Too late," she said. "I'll meet you outside as soon as I can."

"I'm not leaving without you," he said.

"You have to," she said. "Go. Now."

Rucker caught a glimpse of men dressed in the black garb and black turbans indicative of Akund's men as they stormed into the hallway outside of the room Nora was in.

Rucker grabbed his rifle and ducked low, pressing his back to the wall in case the men looked out the window.

The voices sounded loud. He heard Pazir answer and the soft voice of Gulpari. All of the voices faded as if leaving the room. Rucker waited a moment then eased up to the corner of the window and dared to look inside.

His heart sank to the pit of his belly. The room was empty.

He quickly slipped the burqa over his head and tucked his rifle beneath the voluminous folds. Then he walked toward the front of the house, peering through the mesh window the head covering provided.

He squatted low to the ground and peered around the corner.

Half a dozen men in black stood by the gate, each holding an AK-47.

Pazir spoke with their leader. Gulpari, dressed in a blue burqa and carrying her baby, slipped past the men. Behind her was another woman dressed in a burqa.

Nora.

Rucker held his breath, waiting for her to make it past the men.

One of them called out to the women.

Gulpari turned.

Pazir spoke to the man who'd called the women to a halt. He jerked his head toward Gulpari and barked an order.

She nodded, moved closer to Nora and took her hand. Together, they hurried down the street and away from the group of men.

Rucker released the breath he'd been holding and backed away from the corner. He slipped to the rear of the house and pulled himself up over the wall, dropping to the ground on the other side.

Quickly, he headed the same direction Gulpari

and Nora had gone, hoping to intercept them out of sight of Akund's men.

Rucker moved silently on a road parallel with the one Nora and Gulpari had taken. When he passed an alleyway, he glanced to the other street, hoping to catch a glimpse of them.

What he caught sight of were several trucks loaded with more men dressed in black, wielding automatic weapons. The trucks stopped in the street, and the men jumped down and spread out.

Holy hell. Had Abdul Akund brought his entire army to this little town? If so, what were the chances of getting himself and Nora out alive?

Nora moved quickly beside Gulpari as the new mother led her away from the home she and Pazir had brought them to.

How had the Taliban discovered they might be in this small town? Had someone linked the truck to Pazir? For that matter, how had they found Pazir? He'd left his home near the base and moved a long way from there to escape the heavy-handed influence of the Taliban. Yet, here they were, knocking on his door.

"Were they looking for us?" Nora asked Gulpari.

Gulpari's head turned right then left as if she was looking for anyone who might overhear them talking. "Yes. Abdul Akund, their leader, is angry that someone stole from him."

"Do they know Pazir was the one?"

She shook her head. "No. They only knew he'd moved here, the truck carrying their prisoners had headed this way, and they want him to help find the one who betrayed them."

Holy shit. If they found out that Pazir was the one... Hiding Nora and Rucker had put them in grave danger. Hiding them now was their only option. If they were found out now, they'd be dead.

"How did they find you?" Nora whispered.

The woman snorted softly. "Taliban is everywhere."

Then it was only a matter of time before word got back to the Taliban about the truck and who'd taken it. The Taliban would put the pieces together.

Oh, sweet Jesus. Nora bit down hard on her lip. All Pazir and Gulpari wanted was to live in peace, raise their son and be left alone.

The sound of trucks behind them made Nora turn to look over her shoulder.

What she saw made her blood run cold and fear wrap a tight fist around her heart. Several trucks loaded with armed men stopped in the middle of the street. The men dropped down and spread out.

Gulpari ducked right into an alley. Nora followed. She had to get back to Rucker and warn him. But going back would put her in the paths of the men fanning out across the small town.

As they neared the next street an arm reached out from an alcove and grabbed Nora's burqa, yanking it and her into the alcove.

She swallowed a frightened scream and fought to free herself from her captor.

"Nora," a familiar voice said into her ear. "It's me."

Gulpari had stopped as soon as Nora had been pulled away from her.

Nora called out to her, "I'm okay."

Gulpari stepped into the little niche. "We are not safe."

"What about Pazir?" Rucker asked.

"He will meet us on the south edge of town," Gulpari said.

The baby squirmed in her arms and gave a tiny cry.

"They're looking for us, not you," Rucker said. "Go to your husband. We'll go another way."

"But how will you get away from here?" she asked.

"We'll find a way. You and Pazir have done enough for us. You need to get somewhere safe. If you can get word back to the base, let us know you are safe."

She bowed her blue covered head and said, "Peace be with you." Then she turned and hurried away with her baby.

"I feel like we should do something to protect them," Nora said.

"We will. We'll provide a distraction to give them time to get away."

"I wish I could see your expression," Nora said. "You're kidding, right?" She touched his burqa, feeling for his bulletproof vest beneath. "Do you have more of those hand grenades you haven't told me about?"

He chuckled softly. "Sorry. Fresh out of those. But I have some C4 and a remote detonator."

Nora grinned. "Do you always come so well prepared?"

"Only when it counts," he said. "Now, we just need to get to one of those trucks they left parked in the street."

Nora stared at him in his burqa. If they weren't in such dire straits, she'd laugh at how the burqa fit over him. The garment emphasized his broad shoulders and the hem barely came down below his knees. Which meant his black trousers and boots were plain to see. "You will not be able to slip past those men in that getup. On the other hand, I'll have no problem." She squared her shoulders. "What do I need to do to set the charges?"

"No way. You're not stepping out into that street with all those men carrying guns. They've been known to kill women and children. They don't care."

"You can't do it," Nora said. "They'll know

immediately that you're not a woman beneath that burqa. How did you make it this far without being seen?"

"I took the road less traveled...the back alley." He looked around. "Tell you what...I'll create another distraction so that you can plant the explosives without drawing attention."

Nora frowned. "I don't like the sound of that. You're going to put yourself out there to be shot at."

"I'll be fine. But I can't really run in this." He shrugged out of the burqa and stood there, dressed all in black, carrying his rifle with his handgun strapped to his hip.

She gave his body an all-encompassing glance. "Damn, you make it hard for me to walk away."

"I know. You think I'm sexy." He winked, fished in one of his vest pockets and came out with a lump of what appeared to be clay, and a plastic device with an antenna on it.

"This is C4. It's harmless by itself. All you have to do is stick it on what you want destroyed, jam this little device into it and walk away." He handed both to her.

Nora's frown deepened. "Will it blow up when I put the device in the C4?"

"Not until I hit the remote detonator." He held up a little thing that looked like nothing more than a button. "And I'll have the safety on until you get far enough away you won't be hurt."

She raised her eyebrows. "Okay. My life is in your hands."

He nodded, his face grave. "And Pazir and Gulpari and their baby's lives are in ours."

She nodded. "Does it matter which truck?"

"The one in front. Stick it on a wheel, that way it will disable the axle. It won't be going anywhere after that."

Nora drew in a deep breath and let it out slowly. She squared her shoulders and lifted her chin. "I'm ready."

"You don't have to do this."

"With as many men roaming the streets now, none of us will get out of here without drawing attention. We need the diversion."

"Just don't walk down the main street." Rucker pointed to the road he'd come up. "Go back that way. Keep your head down."

Nora had observed the Afghan women. They scurried away from the men and kept their heads down. Considering she was shaking already, that wouldn't be too hard. Avoid the men with the scary guns. Yeah. Easy. Plant the C4 on the wheel of a truck. Even easier.

As she turned away, Rucker grabbed her arm. "I'll watch for you. When you get close, I'll make my move. You'll know it when you hear me."

"Oh, Rucker." She wrapped her arms around him and held on tightly. "Please don't get yourself shot."

"Same goes for you. See those hills?" he pointed to the northwest where hills rose up on the edge of the town. "I'll meet you there."

She nodded. "I'd kiss you, but this darned burqa is in the way."

"I'd love that kiss, but I'll collect on it later."

"Rucker?" Nora said, her heart pounding hard in her chest.

"Yeah, sweetheart?" he held her at arm's length.

"I loved last night," she whispered.

"I did, too," he said and stared down at her.

Then as she turned away, she added beneath her breath, "I love you."

Behind her she could swear she heard him reply in an equally quiet murmur, "I love you, too."

Maybe it was wishful thinking, but it warmed her heart and gave her hope for a future outside this small town in Afghanistan.

She hurried to set her charge and get back to her man in the hills northwest of the town. Everything had to go well. And when it did, they'd figure things out on the other side. Where there was a will and love, there had to be a way.

CHAPTER 14

HE WATCHED Nora as she headed back into the lion's den of Akund's men. As soon as she'd left his side, Rucker regretted letting her go. They could have made their way through the streets to the hills and hidden until his team could come to his rescue.

They could have gotten away, but Pazir, Gulpari and their baby would still be at risk.

When Nora reached the alley across from where the trucks had stopped, she turned and gave him a thumbs-up.

God, he hoped she'd be okay. He had to trust that the burqa hid her well enough and that she was able to set the charge without being caught.

Knowing he was setting himself up to be target practice for the Taliban, Rucker sucked in a deep breath and turned the opposite direction from Nora. He didn't mind being the diversion, as long as it drew attention away from the woman he was growing to love more with each passing moment.

He slipped through the alley Gulpari and Nora had come down from the main street running through town. In just a few short strides he'd be at that street where the trucks had parked, and the men had dismounted.

"Sloan, this is Dash, do you copy?" a voice said into the earbuds he'd almost forgotten he'd worn.

"Dash? Where are you guys?" he whispered.

"We set down on the other side of the hill from the town we located you in. I take it you still have your tracking device in your pocket?"

"I do." He'd come to the corner of a building on the street. Men were working their way toward him, going into houses along the way, rousting the inhabitants. "How many you got with you?"

"Our eight-man team and a backup of a dozen Rangers. As we were coming over the top of the hill, we noticed a couple of truckloads of Taliban heading your way. I take it they made it to town?"

"They did. We were just about to light up their lives."

"We?" Dash asked.

"Me and Nora," Rucker said. Having over twenty men there to support them changed everything.

Except one thing.

Nora would be getting close to the main street waiting for him to start the show.

Damn.

He had no way of telling her to abort the mission. If he didn't create a diversion immediately, the Taliban insurgents would question why she was hanging out on the streets. They'd find it odd when she didn't answer and figure out that she wasn't an Afghan woman after all.

Damn. Damn. Damn.

"About to stir up a hornets nest. You guys close enough to cover my ass?"

"On the northwest edge of the town now, moving in."

"If all goes according to plan, you should see me and Nora running your direction and hear a big bang."

"Gotcha."

"Send a squad to the south side of town. A young couple with a baby need your help. The man's name is Pazir. They helped us get here, now they're in trouble. If you could pick them up, you'll save their lives."

"Sending a squad their way," Dash said.

"Thanks." Rucker glanced around the corner at the six or more men heading his direction. "Going in."

Holding his rifle in his hands, he flipped the safety switch off and tapped the thirty-round magazine for luck and ran out into the street, yelling and firing off several rounds into the air

He didn't spend more than a couple of seconds

crossing the road before he ducked back into the alley on the other side and ran for all he was worth.

"Fuck, Rucker, what the hell are you trying to do?"

"Creating a diversion," he said, running to the next street where he turned right and cut around the next walled home and turned left and circled back toward the trucks and Nora.

Shouts echoed off the buildings behind him. The diversion had the men racing to find the American shooting at them.

They wouldn't expect him to run back in the direction of their trucks. At least, that was what Rucker was banking on.

He made it all the way back to the alley crossing that led to the trucks when he saw a blue burqa turn into the same alley.

Nora.

A rush of relief was quickly followed by a punch in the gut of fear. A man wearing the black garb of the Taliban insurgents, topped by a black turban with a red-checkered cloth woven into it, lunged from around the corner. He grabbed Nora's arm, pulling her to a stop. Then he ripped off her head covering, exposing her blond hair.

She struggled to shake free of his grip, but he held tight.

The man shouted, raising the alarm, and wrapped his arm around her neck in a choke hold. It all went down so fast, that by the time Rucker raised his rifle, he couldn't fire on the man without hitting Nora. And if he wasn't mistaken, the man was the one they'd been after since they'd arrived in country.

Abdul Akund.

"Do it!" Nora yelled.

Rucker reached into his pocket for the detonator. If he didn't set it off, any of the men Akund had with him would surround him and keep him safe, taking Nora with him.

If he set it off, Nora could be hurt in the explosion. She was too close to the trucks.

The options whipped through his mind in milliseconds.

Nora shouted again. "Do it!" Then she rammed her elbow into Akund's gut.

He bent double, loosening his hold on her long enough for her to run deeper into the alley, dive to the ground and cover her head.

Akund pulled a handgun from a holster at his side.

With the detonator switch curled into his palm, Rucker aimed his rifle and fired at Akund, striking him in the chest.

The man fell backward, his gun falling from his hands.

Knowing he only had seconds before Akund's men appeared in the alley, Rucker flipped the safety switch on the detonator and pressed the button.

The explosion shook the earth beneath his feet. The concussion rang in his ears, but it couldn't be helped.

Debris from the truck and the building around them blasted into the air and rained down on him.

Covering his head and neck, Rucker ran to Nora, helped her to her feet and raced back the way he'd come, heading for the northwest side of the small town and his team of Delta Forces.

He swung wide of the main street, hoping to avoid most of the Taliban insurgents.

"I take it that was your party you started," Dash said into Rucker's ear.

"Yup. On our way to intercept the team."

"Do you have your nurse?" Dash asked.

"I do." Rucker responded.

At that moment, a Taliban soldier ran out in front of him, headed back toward the center of the explosion.

Rucker aimed and fired before the other man had a chance to pull the trigger first.

Nora stumbled, and would have fallen, but he reached out with one hand, steadied her and kept running.

"We've engaged," Dash reported. "Four down and counting."

"Swinging wide to avoid getting caught in the crossfire," Rucker said.

"We'll be watching for you."

"We're easy to spot. The nurse is in a blue burqa."

"Good to know," Dawg said. "Got you in my sights."

Even knowing their best sniper was covering them, Rucker still didn't slow down until he was certain they were well behind friendly lines.

"Got you in my sights," Tank said. "Take cover! You have a bogey on your left."

Rucker grabbed Nora's arm and dove behind a building, taking her with him. A bullet hit the dirt and stick corner. Dust and chinks of mud hit them, but the bullet missed.

"Got him. Keep coming, you're almost there," Tank said. "I'll cover from the ground."

"And I've got you from above," Dawg said.

With his team looking out for him, Rucker ran with Nora at his side until they reached the north-west edge of town.

For the last hundred yards, they hadn't run into any of the Taliban insurgents.

Rucker pulled Nora behind a building and stopped.

She doubled over, struggling to catch her breath. "We did it," she said between gasps.

Rucker nodded and tugged her hand, dragging her into his arms. Then he kissed her hard, every emotion roaring through him into the meeting of their lips. He understood that this could be the last time they shared a kiss.

She clung to him, her chest heaving, breathing with him. When they both had to fill their lungs, she flung her head back and sucked in air.

Rucker held her for as long as he could while gunfire sounded. It started off as a barrage, tapering off to the occasional burst until the noise stopped all together.

"We got Pazir and his family," Dash reported. "Arranging for extraction now."

Rucker kissed Nora's forehead. "Pazir and his family are safe. We'll transport them out with the rest of us."

"I'm so glad." Nora smiled, tears welling in her eyes. "But what will happen with them now? The Taliban will know they've betrayed them."

"They'll be taken back to the base where we'll provide them protection until we can figure out how to keep them safe," Rucker said.

The Rangers stayed in the town to help the locals clean up.

The Delta Team loaded into a Black Hawk with Nora, Pazir, Gulpari and the baby. As they waited to take off, Dash said, "We have a positive ID on Abdul Akund's body," he grinned. "Good job, Ruck."

"It was him or Lieutenant Michaels." Rucker shook his head. "It really wasn't an option."

"Considering he was our mission, I guess we'll get clearance to return to Texas," Lance said.

"Where in Texas?" Nora asked.

"Fort Hood. The armpit of the Army," Blade said.

"You're leaving soon, aren't you?" Dash asked.

She nodded. "Going back to Fort Carson, Colorado."

Blade moaned. "Sounds like heaven. We're going from one hot location back to another."

Fort Carson did sound like heaven to Rucker. Anywhere Nora was sounded like heaven. Too bad she wasn't going to Fort Hood.

Rucker wondered if he could get reassigned to a Delta Force team out of Colorado. He'd have to check into that. Then again, he'd hate to leave his team. They were like brothers to him. He wondered how hard it would be for Nora to get orders to come to Fort Hood.

Would she do that for him?

Hell, he'd better start looking into Fort Carson. It wouldn't be fair for her to make sacrifices for him. He had to be equally willing to make sacrifices for her.

Hell, he didn't even know if she was that interested in continuing a relationship with him. What they'd shared could just have been a fling she had no intention of extending past the borders of Afghanistan.

That was a depressing thought. Especially when their time together was quickly coming to an end. He had to get her alone and ask her what she thought of them. Did they have any kind of future? Did she want to see him again? He sure as hell wanted to see her.

The thrill of achieving their team goal paled next to the thought of losing Nora. He couldn't let that occur. If she was willing, he'd move heaven and earth to make them happen.

NORA SAT in the back of the helicopter, leaning against Rucker's broad shoulder. She laid her hand on the seat between them, and he covered hers with his, their gear and clothing hiding the fact. It would be bad if they were caught, but after what she'd been through and what she'd experienced with Rucker, she was at the point of not giving a damn about her Army career.

She wanted to be with Rucker. Too bad they were both heading back to different forts in the States. Fort Carson was a long way from Fort Hood. How could they see each other? Long distance relationships were difficult for people with established commitments. They hadn't even been on a date.

When they landed at the base, they met with Central Command's Special Operations commander where they debriefed him on the operation that had resulted in the neutralization of Abdul Akund. Nora was included in the debriefing since she'd been there through it all, and she had more to add.

"When the children and I were held in that

building by Akund's men, another man came to *inspect* the children the Taliban leader had procured. He was purchasing them."

"That sounds like Akund's modus operandi," the Spec Ops commander said. "He made good money with human trafficking and bounties on our American special operations men."

Nora frowned. "Who paid him to do that?"

"We don't have proof, but we think it might be the Russians," the Spec Ops commander said. "What can you tell us about the man who came to make the purchase of those children?"

Nora's frown deepened. "He was a westerner. By his accent, I'd say he was either American or Canadian."

The Spec Ops Commander exchanged a glance with the base commander. "Sounds like we have some intelligence gathering to do. This is the closest we've gotten to finding out who the buyers are for the people being sold." He turned back to Nora. "Can you describe him?"

She shook her head. "It was dark in the building, with only Akund's flashlight to go by. And the man wore a safari-style hat pulled down low over his forehead. Wish I could help more, but he was only there for a short time. You might try tracking the men and vehicles he sent to collect the children."

"Funny thing about that," the Spec Ops

commander said. "By the time we got back to the building site, those vehicles were gone."

Rucker's brow twisted. "After we disabled them with our grenades?"

The commander nodded. "Gone. With nothing left to give us a clue as to where they'd come from or where they'd gone."

"Whoever it is has some resources if they were able to get those trucks out of there that quickly," Rucker said.

The Special Operations commander reached out a hand to Rucker. "Good job, Sergeant Sloan, on bringing down one of the Taliban's ugliest leaders." He turned to Nora. "And thank you for your part in that. Your actions were commendable. If there's anything I can do for you, you let me know."

She nodded. "Thank you, sir. Right now, all I want is a shower and something to eat."

He laughed. "That can be arranged."

Nora left the briefing room alone while the Delta Force soldiers continued the rest of their debrief. After all that had happened and being with Rucker for more than twenty-four hours, it was a bit of a letdown to walk back to her quarters alone. When she pushed through the door, Beth was there, decorating the room with a homemade chain garland of white printer paper and a big sign taped to the wall.

WELOME BACK AND BON VOYAGE.

"Nora! I'm so glad you're back and okay." She rushed to Nora and hugged her tight.

Tears slipped from Nora's eyes and down her cheeks.

"Oh, sweetie. You're okay, aren't you? Those bastard Taliban assholes didn't hurt you, did they?" Beth set her at arm's length and studied her face.

"No. I'm okay, other than a few broken fingernails." She gave her friend a weak and less convincing smile. "It's just that I'm leaving, and I won't see...my friends anymore."

"You mean, you won't see that hot Delta you've been mooning over since you met him." Beth raised her eyebrows. "Did I hear right? You two spent the past day and night together...did things get serious between you?"

Nora looked down at her wrecked hands and more tears slipped down her cheeks. "I leave for Fort Carson tomorrow, and his unit is shipping back to Fort Hood anytime. What are the chances we'll see each other again?"

"The good thing is that things aren't quite as strict back in the States. As long as you're not seeing each other on duty, and you're not in the same chain of command, you can't be court-marshalled for dating an enlisted man. As long as you have no influence over his promotions, evaluations or assignments, you should be all right."

"I'm in the medical field. I would have nothing to do with all that. But we'll be at different posts so very far from each other. And I don't even know if he'll want to see me after we redeploy to the States." The tears fell in earnest now. "Oh, Beth. How could I fall for someone now? I'm heading back to my old unit. Who knows where they'll send me next? It could be even farther than Colorado. I could be stationed in Alaska!"

"Speaking of which, you got mail today. It looks official. You might want to open it. Maybe it's your orders for your next assignment." Beth handed her an envelope that did look official.

Nora shook her head. "It's probably nothing but a reminder to invest in their savings plan." She tore open the envelope and pulled out an official document.

She read the page, her heart slamming hard against her chest, her breath catching in her throat.

Beth frowned. "What? Did they find out you've been seeing a hunky Delta?" When Nora didn't respond, Beth stepped closer and looked over her shoulder at the document. Then she laughed out loud. "What were the chances? What were the flippin' chances? Girl, you need to invest in some lottery tickets, right now."

"I'm going to Fort Hood," she whispered. She looked up, meeting Beth's gaze, and grinned from ear to ear. "I'm going to Fort Hood!" Then her smile faded, and a frown pulled at her brow. "What if he doesn't want to see me stateside?"

Beth crossed her arms over her chest. "Sweetie, you have a day to find out. I suggest you ask him."

Nora rushed for the door, the paper still in her hands.

"I meant after a shower and food. Hell, he might still be with his unit in the debriefing," Beth called out behind her.

Nora didn't care. She had to know. She ran across the base toward the building where she'd been debriefed.

The Delta Force team was just coming out, Rucker leading the others. He had his back to her, talking to one of his buddies. "I have to see her before she leaves. Stall the CO. Tell him I had to go to the latrine or that I'm sick and I'll be there as soon as I can."

"He's gonna be pissed," Dash said.

"I don't care. I have to see Nor—Lieutenant Michaels."

Dash laughed. "Well, turn around and you will."

"Huh," Rucker said and then turned to find Nora standing behind him.

"Sergeant Sloan, if you have a minute, I'd like to discuss something with you," she said in her most official tone.

He popped a salute and nodded. "Yes, ma'am." He shot a glance over his shoulder. "Cover for me."

"I've got your six," Dash said.

Rucker joined Nora as she turned to walk away from the team of Delta Force Operatives.

"I'm glad you came back. I want you to know—"

"I have some news—" she said at the same time. She laughed and said, "You go first."

"I don't want you to go until you give me your phone number or some way I can reach you when we get back to the States. I want to see you again." He started to take her hand, but then put his behind his back. "I want to touch you," he whispered. "I want to hold you and kiss you. What we have isn't over. It can't be. If I have to, I'll ask for a transfer to Fort Carson. Just say you want to see me again. Please."

Nora raised her hand to touch his face, stopped halfway and put her hands behind her back just like he had to keep from touching him. "I want to see you. I don't want this to end. But don't put in for Fort Carson."

"How can we see each other if we're so far apart? I'll miss my team, but I want to be with you."

"You don't have to go to Fort Carson." She held up the document in her hand. "I'm being transferred to Fort Hood."

"What?" He grabbed the copy of her orders and read them. When he looked up, a big grin spread across his face. "Hot damn!"

Nora glanced around.

Rucker's Delta team were all standing there,

watching what was taking place between Nora and Rucker.

"Well, we all want to know what the good news is, too," Tank shouted.

"She's going to Fort Hood."

A cheer went up from his team, making Nora's cheeks heat.

"Does everyone on your team know we're…" she shrugged, "you know?"

"If they didn't know, they do now. But there are no eyewitnesses to any transgressions," he lowered his voice and added, "and I don't kiss and tell." He handed her orders back to her. "Ma'am, congratulations on your new assignment. I hope to run into you in the great state of Texas."

Nora nodded, fighting the smile tugging at the corners of her lips. "Thank you for saving my life." She left him standing there and practically skipped all the way back to her quarters. Going back to the States would be fabulously wonderful because she would be going back to Rucker.

And he wanted her as much as she wanted him.

Now that she knew, she couldn't wait to go home.

She hugged herself since she couldn't hug Rucker yet. But she would soon.

EPILOGUE

THREE MONTHS later

"RUCKER, I know what our deck looks like," Nora said. He was always wanting to surprise her with something.

They'd moved into a cute little house in Killeen, Texas, outside of Fort Hood a month ago, after dating for only six weeks. "You don't have to make me hide my eyes to take me out there. Unless you've stained it. Ooh. In which case, I can't wait to see it."

Was that a giggle she heard? Were there other people on her back deck? Was it her birthday and she'd forgotten about it?

"Sorry to disappoint you, sweetheart. I didn't stain the deck. But I do have something even better you're going to like," he said. He untied the handkerchief he'd knotted at the back of her head and pulled it free. "Surprise."

She blinked at the brightness of the Texas sun, and then focused on the faces around her.

Mac with his reddish-brown hair and green eyes that made the ladies melt.

Blade's blue eyes watched her intently, his black hair slicked back from his forehead neatly for the first time since Nora could remember.

Dawg stood next to Blade, his warm brown eyes smiling at her. He didn't say much, but those eyes seemed to take it all in. That must be why he was such a good sniper. He saw more than the others.

Tank stood next to Bull, as if vying for who was the tallest and most muscular. They were smiling at her, which made her wonder why. Was her shirt on inside out and she hadn't noticed?

Lance nodded, his gray eyes twinkling. Only a year or two older than the others, he already had graying temples, making him the "old man" of the team.

Dash stepped forward, his lips twisting in a wry grin. "Haven't you noticed yet?" he asked and stepped to the side so that she could see more clearly behind him. "We have special guests."

Nora gasped and pressed a hand to her mouth. "Pazir, Gulpari, oh sweet heaven, you made it here." She rushed forward and hugged the pair and their three-month-old baby.

Tears slipped from Nora's eyes and trailed down her cheeks. "I'm so happy the government granted you asylum. And so quickly."

"We have one more surprise for you," Pazir said. He nodded to Dash, who again stepped aside to reveal yet one more guest.

A little girl wearing a pretty new dress like any other dress a child would wear in the U.S. stood there.

Nora dropped to her knees and held out her arms, tears rolling down her cheeks in earnest. "Taara." She pulled the little girl into her arms and held her tight. "Oh, sweet, baby girl. I can't believe you're here."

Pazir nodded. "We had heard you favored one of the children you helped save. Gulpari and I took her into our home while we waited for your government's approval of our move to the US. We have adopted her and will raise her as our own. You are welcome to visit whenever you like."

"Thank you," she said, a lump lodged firmly in her throat. "You've made my day complete." Nora look up into Rucker's eyes. "Best surprise ever," she said with what little air she could push past her vocal cords.

"I hope not, because I have one more." Rucker pulled a small box out of his front pocket, dropped down on one knee and looked up at her. "Nora Michaels, you are the bravest, most caring and sexiest woman I know. I can't promise that I'll always be here for you, physically, and I'll probably miss some key family events, and I won't always be here to mow the lawn. But I *can* promise that I will do my best to make you happy, and hopefully, fill our house with children, mow the lawn when I'm here and love you forever. Would you do me the greatest honor of all and be my wife?"

She dropped down on her own knees, the tears flowing all over again. "Sweetheart, you had me at mow the lawn. I love you, Rucker Sloan, and yes, I will be your wife."

A cheer went up all around them as Rucker kissed Nora and sealed the deal on a life full of love, laughter and happily ever after.

THE END

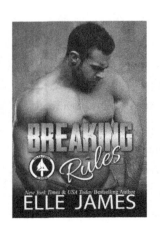

Thank you for reading BREAKING SILENCE. The Delta Force Strong Series continues with BREAKING RULES.

Ryan "Dash" Hayes has a penchant for breaking the rules. If it's for the right reasons, and he doesn't get caught, he won't hesitate. To him, rules are guidelines to be used to keep the sheep in line, not him. But his commander is willing to give him the benefit of the doubt because he's good at his job as a Delta Force Operative. Fast, effective and willing to sacrifice his life to save others.

After her singing partner is killed in a bus crash, Sunny Daye joins the USO. What better way to punish herself for surviving than to put herself at risk in a country full of conflict? When attempts are made to kidnap her, she's given a choice…leave the country or accept a bodyguard for the remainder of her tour.

Enter Dash, the cocky, irreverent Delta Force soldier who seems to show up at the best/worst times to save the day.

Okay, if she has to have a bodyguard, she has a few rules he must follow:

One - Hands off

Two - No kissing

Three - No falling in love with the talent

With a grin and a wink, Dash agrees to her terms. But then Dash has never met a rule he wasn't willing to break.

BREAKING RULES

Interested in more military romance stories? Subscribe to my newsletter and receive the Military Heroes Box Set

Subscribe Here

HELLFIRE, TEXAS

HELLFIRE SERIES BOOK #1

New York Times & *USA Today*
Bestselling Author

ELLE JAMES

All hell breaks loose when a firefighter
rescues a runaway

Hellfire,
Texas

A Hellfire Story

NEW YORK TIMES BESTSELLING AUTHOR

ELLE JAMES

CHAPTER 1

THE HOT JULY sun beat down on the asphalt road. Shimmering heat waves rose like mirages as Becket Grayson drove the twenty miles home to Coyote Creek Ranch outside of Hellfire, Texas. Wearing only a sweat-damp T-shirt and the fire retardant pants and boots of a firefighter, he couldn't wait to get home, strip, and dive into the pool. Although he'd have to hose down before he clouded the water with the thick layer of soot covering his body from head to toe.

The Hellfire Volunteer Firefighter Association met the first Saturday of every month for training in firefighting, rescues, and first responder care. Today had been particularly grueling in the late summer swelter. Old Lady Mersen graciously donated her dilapidated barn for structural fire training and rescue.

All thirty volunteers had been on hand to participate. Though hot, the training couldn't have gone better. Each volunteer got a real taste of how fast an old barn would go up in flames, and just how much time they had to rescue any humans or animals inside. Some had the opportunity to exercise the use of SCBA, self-contained breathing apparatus, the masks and oxygen tanks that allowed them to enter smoke-filled buildings, limiting exposure and damage to their lungs. Other volunteers manned the fire engine and tanker truck, shuttling water from a nearby pond to the portable tank deployed on the ground. They unloaded a total of five tanks onto the barn fire before it was completely extinguished. With only one tanker truck, the shuttle operation slowed their ability to put out the fire, as the blaze rebuilt each time they ran out of water in the holding pool. They needed at least two tanker trucks in operation to keep the water flowing. As small as the Hellfire community was, the first engine and tanker truck would never have happened without generous donations from everyone in the district *and* a government grant. But, they had an engine that could carry a thousand, and a tanker capable of thirty-five hundred gallons. Forty-five hundred gallons was better than nothing.

Hot, tired, and satisfied with what he'd learned about combating fire without the advantages of a city fire hydrant and unlimited water supply, Becket had learned one thing that day. Firefighting involved a lot more than he'd ever imagined. As the Fire Chief said, all fires were different, just like people were different. Experience taught you the similarities, but you had to expect the unexpected.

Two miles from his turnoff, Becket could almost taste the ice-cold beer waiting in the fridge and feel the cool water of the ranch swimming pool on his skin.

A puff of dark smoke drifted up from a stalled vehicle on the shoulder of the road ahead. The puff grew into a billowing cloud, rising into the air.

Becket slowed as he neared the disabled vehicle.

A black-haired woman stood in the V of the open driver's door, attempting to push the vehicle off the road. She didn't need to worry about getting it off the road so much as getting herself away from the smoke and fire before the gas tank ignited and blew the car to pieces.

A hundred yards away from the potential disaster, Becket slammed on his brakes, shifted into park, and jumped out of his truck. "Get away from the car!" he yelled, running toward the idiot woman. "Get away before it explodes!"

The woman shot a brief glance back at him before continuing on her mission to get the car completely off the road and into the bone-dry grass.

Becket ran up behind her, grabbed her around the

middle, and hauled her away from the now-burning vehicle.

"Let go of me!" she screamed, tearing at his hands. "I have to get it off the road."

"Damn it, lady, it's not safe." Not knowing when the tank would ignite, he didn't have time to argue. Becket spun her around, threw her over his shoulder in a fireman's carry, and jogged away from the burning vehicle.

"I have to get it off the road," she said, her voice breaking with each jolt to her gut.

"Leave it where it is. I'll call in the fire department, they'll have the fire out before you know it. In the meantime, that vehicle is dangerous." He didn't stop or put her down until he was back behind his truck.

He set her on her feet, but she darted away from him, running back toward the vehicle, her long, jet-black hair flying out behind her.

Becket lunged, grabbed her arm, and jerked her back. "Are you crazy?"

"I can't leave it in the road," she sobbed. "Don't you see? He'll find it. He'll find me!" She tried prying his fingers free of her arm.

He wasn't letting go.

"The fire will ignite the gas tank. Unless you want to be fried like last year's turkey, you need to stand clear." He held her back to his chest, forcing her to view the fire and the inherent danger.

She sagged against him, her body shaking with the force of her sobs. "I have to hide it."

"Can I trust you to stay put?"

She nodded, her hair falling into her face.

"I'm making a call to the Hellfire Volunteer Firefighters Association."

Before he finished talking, she was shaking her head. "No. You can't. No one can know I'm here."

"Why?" He settled his hands on her shoulders and was about to turn her to face him when an explosion rocked the ground.

Becket grabbed the woman around the waist.

She yelped and whimpered as Becket ducked behind the tailgate of his pickup, and waited for the debris to settle. Then he slowly rose.

Smoke and fire shot into the air. Where the car had been now was a raging inferno. Black smoke curled into the sky.

"Sweetheart, I won't have to call 911. In the next fifteen minutes, this place will be surrounded by firefighters."

Her head twisted left and right as she attempted to pry his hands away from her waist. "You're hurting me."

He released her immediately. "The sheriff will want a statement from you."

"No. I can't." Again, she darted away from him. "I have to get as far away from here as possible."

Becket snagged her arm again and whipped her

around. "You can't just leave the scene of a fire. There will be an investigation." He stared down at her, finally getting a look at her. "Do I know you?"

"I don't…" The young woman glanced up, eyes narrowing. She reached up a hand and rubbed some of the soot off his face. Recognition dawned and her eyes grew round. "Becket? Becket Grayson?"

He nodded. "And I know I should know you, but I can't quite put my finger on it."

Her widened eyes filled with tears, and she flung her arms around his neck. "Oh, dear God. Becket!"

He held her, struggling to remember who she was.

Her body trembled, her arms like clamps around his neck.

"Hey." Surprised by her outburst, Becket patted her back. "It's going to be okay."

"No, it's not," she cried into his sweat-dampened shirt, further soaking it with her tears. "No, it's not."

His heart contracted, feeling some of the pain in her voice. "Yes, it is. But you have to start by telling me who you are." He hugged her again, then loosened the arms around his neck and pushed her to arms' length. "Well?"

The cheek she'd rested against his chest was black with soot, her hair wild and tangled. Familiar green eyes, red-rimmed and awash with tears, looked up at him. "You don't remember me." It was a statement, not a question.

"Sorry. You look awfully familiar, but I'm just not

making the connection." He smiled gently. "Enlighten me."

"I'm Kinsey Phillips. We used to be neighbors."

His confusion cleared, and he grinned. "Little Kinsey Phillips? The girl who used to hang out with Nash and follow us around the ranch, getting into trouble?"

Sniffling, she nodded.

Becket shook his head and ran his gaze over her from head to toe. "Look at you, all grown up." He chuckled. "Although, you didn't get much taller."

She straightened to her full height. "No. Sadly, I stopped growing taller when I was thirteen."

"Well, Little Kinsey..." He pulled her into the curve of his arm and faced the burning mess that had been her car. "What brings you back to Hellfire? Please tell me you didn't come to have your car worked on by my brother, Rider. I'm afraid there's no hope for it."

She bit her lip, and the tremors of a few moments before returned. "I didn't know where else to go. But I think I've made a huge mistake."

Her low, intense tone made Becket's fists clench, ready to take on whatever had her so scared. "Why do you say that?"

"He'll find me and make me pay."

"Who will find you?" Becket demanded, turning her to face him again.

She looked up at him, her bottom lip trembling. "My ex-boyfriend."

KINSEY SHUDDERED, her entire body quaking with the magnitude of what she'd done. She'd made a bid for freedom. If she didn't distance herself from the condemning evidence, all of her efforts to escape the hell she'd lived in for the past year, would be for nothing.

Sirens sounded in the distance, shaking her out of her stupor and spurring her to action. "You can't let them question me." She turned toward the still-burning vehicle. "It's bad enough this is the first place he'll look for me."

"Who is your boyfriend?"

"Ex-boyfriend," Kinsey corrected. "Dillon Massey."

"Name's familiar. Is he from around here?"

Kinsey shook her head, scanning the immediate area. "No, he's from Waco. He played football for Baylor a couple years ago, and he's playing for the Cowboys now."

"Massey, the quarterback?"

"Yes." She nodded, and then grabbed Becket's hands. "Please, you can't let anyone know I'm here. Dillon will make them think I'm crazy, and that I need him to look out for me." Kinsey pulled herself up straight. "I'm not. I've never been more lucid in my life. I had to get away."

Becket frowned. "Why?"

She raised her blouse, exposing the bruises on her ribs. "And there are more. Everywhere most people won't see."

His brows dipping lower, Becket's nostrils flared. "Bastard."

"You have no idea." Kinsey glanced toward the sound of the sirens. "Please. Let me hide. I can't face anyone."

"Who does the car belong to?"

Her jaw tightened. "Me. I'm surprised it got me this far. The thing has barely been driven in over a year."

"Why not?"

"He parked it in his shed and hid the keys. I found them early this morning, while he was passed out drunk."

"When they conduct the investigation, they'll trace the license plates."

She tilted her chin. "I removed them."

"Did you leave a purse with your identification inside the vehicle?"

"No. I didn't bring anything. I knew I'd have to start over with a new name."

"If there's anything left of the Vehicle Identification Number, they can track it through the system."

Glancing at the empty road, the sirens sounding

closer, Kinsey touched Becket's arm. "It will take time for them to find the details. By then, I could be halfway across the country. But right now, I can't talk to the sheriff or the firemen. If anyone knows I'm here, that knowledge could find its way into some police database and will allow Dillon to locate me. He has connections with the state police, the district courts, and who knows what other organizations." She shook her head. "I won't go back to him."

"Okay, okay." Becket rounded to the passenger side and opened the door. "Get in."

She scrambled in, hands shaking, her heart beating so fast she was sure it would explode like the car. Kinsey glanced out the back window of the truck. The road was still clear. A curve hid them from view for a little longer. "Hurry."

"On it." Dillon fired up the engine and pulled onto the blacktop, flooring the accelerator. They reached the next curve before the rescue vehicles appeared.

Kinsey collapsed against the seat back, her nerves shot and her stomach roiling. "That was close."

"Sweetheart, you don't know just how close. If emergency vehicles hadn't been coming, I would not have left. As dry as it's been, a fire like that could spread too easily, consuming thousands of acres if left unchecked."

"I'm sorry. I wouldn't have asked you to leave the scene, but I know Dillon. The last time I tried to leave, I was caught because he called the state police and had me hauled home."

"Couldn't you have gone to a hospital and asked for a social worker to verify your injuries?" Becket glanced her way, his brows furrowed in a deep V. "Women's shelters are located all over Dallas."

"I tried." She turned toward the window, her heart hurting, reliving the pain of the beating he'd given her when he'd brought her home. He'd convinced the hospital she'd fallen down the stairs. No one wanted to believe the quarterback of an NFL team would terrorize his girlfriend into submission, beating her whenever he felt like it. "Look, you don't need to be involved in this. If you could take me to the nearest truck stop, I'll hitch a ride."

"Where would you go?"

"Wherever the trucker is going."

He shook his head. "Hitchhiking is dangerous."

Kinsey snorted. "It'd be a cakewalk compared to what I've been through."

Becket sat silent, gripping the steering wheel so tightly his knuckles turned white. "Nash is part of the sheriff's department in Hellfire now. Let me call him."

"No!" She shook her head, violently. "You can't report me to the sheriff's department. I told you. Dillon has friends everywhere, even in the state police and Texas Rangers. He'd have them looking for me. If a report popped up anywhere in the state, they'd notify him immediately."

"When was the last time he saw you?"

"Last night. After he downed a fifth of whiskey, Dillon gave me the bruises you saw. I'm sure he slept it off by eight this morning. He'll be looking for me. By now, he's got the state police on the lookout for my car. He probably reported it as stolen. I wouldn't be surprised if he puts out a missing person report, claiming I've been kidnapped." Kinsey sighed. "Take me to the truck stop. I won't have you arrested for helping me."

"I'm not taking you to the truck stop."

Kinsey slid the window down a crack and listened. She couldn't hear the sirens anymore. Her pulse slowed and she allowed herself to relax against the back of the seat.

Becket slowed and turned at the gate to the Coyote Creek Ranch.

The entrance was just as she remembered. Rock columns supported the huge arched sign with the name of the ranch burned into the wood. She'd grown up on the much-smaller ranch next door. The only child of older parents, she'd ride her horse to visit the Graysons. She loved Nash and Rider like the brothers she'd never had. Chance had been a wild card, away more than he was there, and Becket...

As a young teen, Kinsey had the biggest crush on Becket, the oldest of the Graysons. She'd loved his longish blond hair and those startling blue eyes. Even now, covered in soot, his eyes were a bright spot of color on an otherwise-blackened face.

"I can't stay here," she said, looking over her shoulder. "Your wife and children don't need me dragging them through whatever Dillon has in store for me. I guarantee, repercussions will be bad."

"Don't worry about the Graysons. Mom and Dad are in Hawaii, celebrating their 40th anniversary. None of us brothers are married, and Lily's too stubborn to find a man to put up with her."

"What?" Kinsey glanced his way. "Not married? Are the women in this area blind? I practically worshipped you as a child."

Becket chuckled. "I remember you following me around when Nash and Rider were busy. Seems you were always there when I brought a girl out to the ranch."

Her cheeks heated. She'd done her darnedest to be in the way of Becket and his girlfriends. She didn't like it when he kissed and hugged on them. In her dreams, she'd been the one he'd fallen in love with and wanted to marry. But that hadn't happened. He'd dated the prom queen and married her soon after graduation.

"I thought you had married."

"Didn't last."

"Why not?"

"It's a long story."

"If I remember, it's a long driveway up to the ranch house."

Becket paused. For a moment, Kinsey thought he was done talking about his life and failed marriage. Then he spoke again. "After college, Briana wanted me to stay and work for one of the big architecture firms in Dallas. I was okay with the job for a while, but I missed the ranch."

"You always loved being outdoors. I can't imagine you stuck in an office."

He nodded. "Dad had a heart attack four years ago."

"I'm sorry to hear that, but I assume he survived, since they're in Hawaii."

Becket smiled. "He did, but he can't work as hard as he used to."

"So, you came home to run the ranch?"

"Yeah." Becket's gaze remained on the curving drive ahead. "Briana didn't want to leave the social scene. We tried the long-distance thing, but she didn't like it. Or rather, the marriage didn't work for her when she found a wealthy replacement for me."

"Wow. That's harsh."

"Eh. It all worked out for the best. We didn't have children, because she wanted to wait. I like it here. I have satellite internet. I telecommute in the evenings on projects for my old firm, so I stay fresh on what's going on in the industry. During the day, I'm a rancher."

"Sounds like you know what you want out of life." Kinsey sighed and rested her head against the window. "I just want to be free of Dillon."

"What about you? You went to Baylor. Did you graduate?"

"I did. With a nursing degree. I worked in pediatric nursing."

"Did you?"

"For a while. Dillon was still at Baylor when I graduated. When he signed on with the Cowboys, he changed. He said I didn't need to work and badgered me into quitting." Kinsey remembered how much she hated staying at home, and how useless she felt. "I loved my job. The kids were great."

Becket stared at the road ahead. "We leave high school with a lot of dreams and expectations."

"I figured I'd be happily married by now with one or two kids." Kinsey snorted.

"Same here." Becket's lips twisted. "We play the hands we're dealt. How long have you put up with the abuse?"

"Too long." Kinsey stared out the window. "The beatings started when he signed on with the NFL. He'd take me to parties. When his teammates paid too much attention to me, he'd get jealous, drink too much, and hit me when we got back to our place."

"Why didn't you leave him then?"

"In the morning, he'd apologize and promise not to do it again." Her lip pulled back in a sneer. "But, he did. Eventually, he stopped taking me to the parties." Her life would have been so different had she left him the first time he hit her. She'd been a fool to believe he would stop.

"Couldn't you have gone to your family?"

"Each time I mentioned leaving, Dillon flew into a rage and threatened to kill me. Then he took away my car. He said it was for my own good. The car was too old, and needed too much work to drive." At first, Kinsey had thought his action was out of concern for her safety. But her checkbook and credit cards disappeared, and he blamed her for being careless, forcing her to live off whatever pittance of cash he gave her. Without a job, she had no income and became a prisoner in Dillon's home. "He told me I was a terrible driver and shouldn't be on the road. That I'd probably end up crashing into someone."

"The man's a dick."

"Tell me about it." Kinsey bit her lip to keep it from trembling. "I think part of the reason he stopped me from driving was that I'd go to visit my parents. Like he was jealous of how much I loved them, and liked spending time at home. By taking away my car, he left me with no way of getting there. Mom and Dad came up to visit me in Dallas when they could, but after they left, Dillon would stomp around the house, sullen and angry. He'd accuse me of being a mama's girl. If I defended myself, he hit me."

"Your parents were good people," Becket said. "I was sorry to hear of the accident."

Tears slipped from Kinsey's eyes. "They were on their way to visit me, since I couldn't go to them. I think they knew I was in trouble."

"Why didn't you tell them what was going on?"

"I was embarrassed, ashamed, and scared. By then, Dillon was my world. I didn't think I had any other alternatives. And he swore he loved me."

"He had a lousy way of showing it," Becket said through tight lips.

She agreed. Along with the physical abuse, Dillon heaped enough mental and verbal abuse on Kinsey, she'd started to believe him.

You're not smart enough to be a nurse. You'll kill a kid with your carelessness, he'd say.

When her parents died, she'd stumbled around in a fog of grief. Dillon coerced her into signing a power of attorney, allowing him to settle their estate. Before she knew what he'd done, he'd sold her parents' property, lock, stock and barrel, without letting her go through any of their things. He'd put the money in his own account, telling her it was a joint account. She never saw any of the money—never had access to the bank.

Several times over the past few months, she had considered leaving him. But with her parents gone, no money to start over, and no one to turn to, she'd hesitated.

Then, a month ago, he'd beaten her so badly she'd been knocked unconscious. When she came to, she knew she had to get out before he killed her. She stole change out of Dillon's drawer, only a little at a time so he wouldn't notice. After a couple weeks, she had enough for a tank of gas.

Dillon settled into a pattern of drinking, beating her, and passing out. She used the hours he was unconscious to scour the house in search of her keys. She'd begun to despair, thinking he'd thrown them away. Until last night. He'd gone out drinking with his teammates. When he'd arrived home, he'd gone straight to the refrigerator for another beer. He'd forgotten he'd finished off the last bottle the night before and blamed her for drinking the beer. With no beer left in the house, he reached for the whiskey.

With a sickening sense of the inevitable, Kinsey braced herself, but she was never prepared when he started hitting. This time, when he passed out, she'd raided his pockets and the keychain he guarded carefully. On it was the key to her car.

Grabbing the handful of change she'd hoarded, she didn't bother packing clothes, afraid if she took too long, he'd wake before she got her car started and out of the shed.

Heart in her throat, she'd pried open the shed door and climbed into her dusty old vehicle. She'd stuck the key in the ignition, praying it would start. Dillon had charged the battery and started the car the week before, saying it was time to sell it. Hopefully, the battery had retained its charge.

On her second attempt, she pumped the gas pedal and held her breath. The engine groaned, and by some miracle it caught, coughed, and sputtered to life.

Before she could chicken out, before Dillon could stagger through the door and drag her out of the vehicle, she'd shoved the gear shift into reverse and backed out of the shed, scraping her car along the side of Dillon's pristine four-wheel drive pickup, and bounced over the curb onto the street.

She'd made it out, and she wasn't going back.

ABOUT THE AUTHOR

ELLE JAMES also writing as MYLA JACKSON is a *New York Times* and *USA Today* Bestselling author of books including cowboys, intrigues and paranormal adventures that keep her readers on the edges of their seats. When she's not at her computer, she's traveling, snow skiing, boating, or riding her ATV, dreaming up new stories. Learn more about Elle James at www.ellejames.com

Website | Facebook | Twitter | GoodReads | Newsletter | BookBub | Amazon

Or visit her alter ego Myla Jackson at
mylajackson.com
Website | Facebook | Twitter | Newsletter

Follow Me!
www.ellejames.com
ellejames@ellejames.com

ALSO BY ELLE JAMES

Brotherhood Protectors Colorado

SEAL Salvation (#1)

Rocky Mountain Rescue (#2)

Ranger Redemption (#3)

Tactical Takeover (#4)

Shadow Assassin (crossover)

Delta Force Strong

Ivy's Delta (Delta Force 3 Crossover)

Breaking Silence (#1)

Breaking Rules (#2)

Breaking Away (#3)

Breaking Free (#4)

Breaking Hearts (#5)

Iron Horse Legacy

Soldier's Duty (#1)

Ranger's Baby (#2)

Marine's Promise (#3)

SEAL's Vow (#4)

Warrior's Resolve (#5)

Brotherhood Protectors Series

Montana SEAL (#1)

Bride Protector SEAL (#2)

Montana D-Force (#3)

Cowboy D-Force (#4)

Montana Ranger (#5)

Montana Dog Soldier (#6)

Montana SEAL Daddy (#7)

Montana Ranger's Wedding Vow (#8)

Montana SEAL Undercover Daddy (#9)

Cape Cod SEAL Rescue (#10)

Montana SEAL Friendly Fire (#11)

Montana SEAL's Mail-Order Bride (#12)

SEAL Justice (#13)

Ranger Creed (#14)

Delta Force Rescue (#15)

Montana Rescue (Sleeper SEAL)

Hot SEAL Salty Dog (SEALs in Paradise)

Hot SEAL Bachelor Party (SEALs in Paradise)

Brotherhood Protectors Vol 1

The Outrider Series

Homicide at Whiskey Gulch (#1)

Hideout at Whiskey Gulch (#2)

Hellfire Series

Hellfire, Texas (#1)

Justice Burning (#2)

Smoldering Desire (#3)

Hellfire in High Heels (#4)

Playing With Fire (#5)

Up in Flames (#6)

Total Meltdown (#7)

Take No Prisoners Series

SEAL's Honor (#1)

SEAL'S Desire (#2)

SEAL's Embrace (#3)

SEAL's Obsession (#4)

SEAL's Proposal (#5)

SEAL's Seduction (#6)

SEAL'S Defiance (#7)

SEAL's Deception (#8)

SEAL's Deliverance (#9)

SEAL's Ultimate Challenge (#10)

Billionaire Online Dating Service

The Billionaire Husband Test (#1)

The Billionaire Cinderella Test (#2)

The Billionaire Bride Test (#3)

The Billionaire Daddy Test (#4)

The Billionaire Matchmaker Test (#5)

The Billionaire Glitch Date (#6)

The Billionaire Perfect Date (#7) coming soon

The Billionaire Replacement Date (#8) coming soon

The Billionaire Wedding Date (#9) coming soon

Hearts & Heroes Series

Wyatt's War (#1)

Mack's Witness (#2)

Ronin's Return (#3)

Sam's Surrender (#4)

Cajun Magic Mystery Series

Voodoo on the Bayou (#1)

Voodoo for Two (#2)

Deja Voodoo (#3)

Cajun Magic Mysteries Books 1-3

Texas Billionaire Club

Tarzan & Janine (#1)

Something To Talk About (#2)

Who's Your Daddy (#3)

Love & War (#4)

Declan's Defenders

Marine Force Recon (#1)

Show of Force (#2)

Full Force (#3)

Driving Force (#4)

Tactical Force (#5)

Disruptive Force (#6)

Mission: Six

One Intrepid SEAL

Two Dauntless Hearts

Three Courageous Words

Four Relentless Days

Five Ways to Surrender

Six Minutes to Midnight

Ballistic Cowboy

Hot Combat (#1)

Hot Target (#2)

Hot Zone (#3)

Hot Velocity (#4)

SEAL Of My Own

Navy SEAL Survival

Navy SEAL Captive

Navy SEAL To Die For

Navy SEAL Six Pack

Devil's Shroud Series

Deadly Reckoning (#1)

Deadly Engagement (#2)

Deadly Liaisons (#3)

Deadly Allure (#4)

Deadly Obsession (#5)

Deadly Fall (#6)

Thunder Horse Series

Hostage to Thunder Horse (#1)

Thunder Horse Heritage (#2)

Thunder Horse Redemption (#3)

Christmas at Thunder Horse Ranch (#4)

Demon Series

Hot Demon Nights (#1)

Demon's Embrace (#2)

Tempting the Demon (#3)

Lords of the Underworld

Witch's Initiation (#1)

Witch's Seduction (#2)

The Witch's Desire (#3)

Possessing the Witch (#4)